NO BOSS OF MINE

IONA ROSE

RIVER LAURENT

Thank You To

Leanore Elliott
Brittany Urbaniak
Cover Couture
www.bookcovercouture.com

978-1-911608-43-1

INTRODUCTION

Hey there!

Thank you for choosing my book. I sure hope that you love it. I'd hate to part ways once you're done though. So how about we stay in touch?

My newsletter is a great way to discover more about me and my books. Where you'll find frequent exclusive giveaways, sneak previews of new releases and be first to see new cover reveals.

And as a HUGE thank you for joining, you'll receive a FREE book on me!

With love,

Iona

Get Your FREE Book Here

Get Your FREE Book Here

1

FINN

I lean against the balcony wall and take a long pull from the cigarette I bummed off my Grandpa's lawyer. The last time I smoked was when I was nineteen, but today is bad, crazy bad. I've been out here on the balcony for what seems like a lifetime, and I'm almost done with my cigarette, but it's done nothing to calm me down.

I shake my head, partly in disbelief, and partly in anger. My lips twist into a smile. It's not the sort of smile that reaches my eyes. It's bitter. After ninety years on earth, the old man couldn't just let go and enjoy heaven or wherever he has gone.

"You've really fucking done it this time, Grandpa," I mutter under my breath.

I look out over the carefully cultivated grounds of my parents' home, trying to stop the thoughts of my grandpa, who, it seems, has excelled himself and found a way to fuck with me even from beyond the grave.

The wind picks up, rustling the leaves of the tall trees around the edges of the huge lawn. The gardener is cleaning the massive Romanesque marble fountain my father had imported from Italy as a wedding gift for my mother. She is very proud of it.

I caught hell off her for squirting a whole bottle of dish soap into the water when I was seven. I was delighted with the result. I thought it looked magical with bubbles and suds everywhere.

My mother, not so much.

I straighten and take one last drag of the foul cigarette, then crush it out in the ashtray on the glass table behind me.

I should have known something like this was coming. Obviously, not this exact thing, I never could have predicted this one in a million years, but I should have known there would be something. My grandpa has always challenged me, pushed me to be the best version of myself, even when I resisted him, but this? This one is completely, totally, utterly from left field.

Throughout his entire life, he never did anything without a reason. When he asked me to run his company for him seven years ago, I should have guessed there would be a catch, that it was only the first phase of his plan for me.

I guess I was naïve, but when he told me he had terminal cancer and he wanted me to take the helm, I thought maybe I had finally done it. I'd impressed the unimpressible man enough to have him take a back seat and leave me to it. But no, I hadn't. We were at loggerheads the whole time. Ninety-five percent of the time he was wrong, but it was worth the stress for the five percent when he had the better solution.

He's finally done it now though. He's set me a challenge he thought I wouldn't be able to rise to.

"You underestimated me, Grandpa. I see your challenge and I fucking raise you the final victory," I say to him, wherever he is. Then I head towards the doors leading back into the house.

I step back inside the house, and walk through the cooler, air conditioned air of the interior. I make my way quickly towards the large, elegant dining room, which is where my mother, my dad, and Andrew Garfield, my grandpa's lawyer and the executor of his will, are waiting.

My mother usually looks young for her age, but today, her face shows the strain of this meeting. My dad is as stoic as ever, hiding his fury behind a stony mask of neutrality. Anyone who knows him well though, will not fail to see the little tic above his jawbone, a sure sign that he's tightly holding himself from blowing a gasket.

Thank God, he got his share of Grandpa's fortune without having to jump through the hoops I'm having too. Grandpa played it clever. He knew it's not about the money for me. If it were, I'd have walked away a long time ago and told him to stuff it. He's made it about something I feel is mine. Something I've spent the last three years building to the exclusion of everything else.

Hell, I've poured everything I have into this business.

I can't just let go of it, and he fucking knew it. It's my life.

Especially not now, when I'm just about to transition it into the next level and turn it into something amazing.

As I step into the room, Andrew looks at me expectantly. I ignore his eyes and stop off at the dresser to pour myself a glass of iced water from a jug. I don't want the water. I want a very large glass of whisky, but there you have it. I compose my face as I pour the water, then I saunter over to the long table and retake my seat. "Okay, Andrew. Run this thing by me again," I say.

He does it with pleasure. After all, he bills clients, in this case, my grandpa's estate, at five hundred dollars an hour, so he's in no hurry at all.

As he drones on, I start tapping my fingers on the table.

Finally, he gets to the dreaded part. He clears his throat and gets it out, "In order to inherit your grandfather's shares and gain full control of the company, you'll have to marry Ashley Winters, the granddaughter of Walter Winters, who co-founded the company with your grandfather." Andrew stops and watches me over the top of his silver framed glasses.

This had been the point I had walked out of the room before... in furious shock.

"And if I don't?" I ask quietly.

"Then the shares go to the board, being shared equally between them, giving you no voting rights, although your job as CEO will be safe, of course."

My grandpa knew how I would view this. What's the point in being the CEO of a company if you can't make any important or risky decisions? I had gotten the company this far because I'd made decisions other men wouldn't. This deal would suit some people, but I am not one of those people. And Grandpa knew this.

I had begun to take the company in a completely new direction, one my grandpa allowed to happen, but it was clear the board seemed wary. They still are. Given half the chance, they would crash all my hard work and just keep the company ticking along at its present state. They don't understand that if the company doesn't grow now, it will be a dead duck in today's digital world.

Andrew looks at me calmly.

The choice is simple. Marry Walter's granddaughter or stand back and let all of the work be for nothing and watch from afar as the company slowly disintegrates until there's nothing left of it. "And this Ashley. She's agreed to this?" I ask.

"Not exactly," Andrew mutters, looking uncomfortable for the first time since he arrived here in his expensive car and his expensive suit. "Ms. Winters has no idea she is part of this clause."

"What?" I explode.

"You'll have to... um... talk her into it."

"I don't fucking believe this," I mutter and shoot to my feet. "So what's in it for her?" I demand. "Why would she agree to this—this— madness?"

"I'm afraid I can't help you with that one, Finn. Your grandfather's answer when I asked him the same question was that you'll use your natural charm."

"Oh well, that should be easy enough then," I say sarcastically.

"Financial inducements do help," Andrew suggests delicately.

The truth is, he could be right. If I agree to this, and get this Ashley girl to agree to it, then I can make Ashley the sort of financial offer she won't be able to refuse.

"Mr. Garfield," my mother burst out, ever formal, even though Andrew has told her to call him Andrew a hundred times. "This is completely ridiculous. The terms are archaic and are just a sign of that old fool trying to control not just Finn's life, but the life of this poor girl's too. It's not realistic and there must be some way around it."

"There isn't," Andrew says. "I'm afraid Finn's grandfather made this particular specification watertight, Helen. He's even closed the senility loophole by getting a certification that he was of sound mind from a psychiatrist."

"We'll go to court. Fight it. No court will uphold such a silly clause," my mom fumes fiercely.

Andrew looks a little surprised, although he hides it well, covering the tiny flash of emotion by clearing his throat and pushing his glasses up his nose. "You could try it, but I guarantee you will lose. The will is clear and has been through all of the correct channels. And even if you do win the case, there will be nothing left to win."

"What do you mean?" my father asks.

He's been silent throughout the rest of the meeting and we all turn to look at him.

"The terms are clear," Andrew explains. "If the will is contested, the company is to go on the market immediately and be sold for one hundred thousand dollars and it cannot be bought by any of the family or by any proxy of this family."

"What?" my mother cries in disbelief.

"But it's worth three hundred times that," my father exclaims.

"Actually, it's worth three hundred and seventy nine times that." Andrew nods. "And that's the point. The company will be sold for one hundred thousand dollars, and by the time the fees and taxes are paid, Finn will stand to inherit around two thousand dollars."

"Well damn," my father says, shaking his head. He tries to hide it, but there is grudging admiration in his voice at how truly wily the old man was. "He's really got this sewn-up, hasn't he?"

"So it would seem," Andrew replies.

"Look Mr. Garfield, I know the man was my father-in-law, and I hate to say this, but he was clearly insane when he wrote this will. Finn has worked so hard bettering this company and quite frankly, he deserves better," my mom states.

"I'm not here to debate what your son deserves, Helen," Andrew replies. "I'm here to see to it that your father-in-law's will is adhered to. He wasn't insane when the will was drafted, as three separate psychiatrists attested to, in the event you tried to pull that card." He turns his attention back to me. "The choice is simple Finn. You remain at the company as an employee with a big office, an obscene salary, and a fancy title, or you marry Ashley Winters and run the company as you see fit. That's really all there is to say on the matter. I'll leave you my card and you can call me when you have made your decision. You have three business days to decide, and if I don't hear from you within that time frame, then the company goes on the market."

"Three days," my mother gasps incredulously. "That's not enough time to bake a fruit cake."

"I'll do it," I say. I never had any real doubt in my mind. I would do it. I would show my grandpa I am worthy one last time and I would keep the company I'd turned around with my blood, sweat, and tears, if it was the last thing I ever did.

"Finn, you don't have to do this," my father cautions. "Those aren't the only two choices. You can walk into any firm in the city, and get a real job where you have real power and real responsibilities. Better still, you can start your own. Between you and me, we have enough."

"I know that, Dad, but it wouldn't be the same. I can't walk away. Not after I have given everything to this company. I can't see it fall into the hands of a board who knows nothing about the current market trends and watch them run it into the ground."

"But you've never even met this girl," my mom cries.

I shrug. "It will only be a marriage of convenience." I don't add on the rest of what I'm thinking. It'll be a quick wedding, a quiet affair no one needs to know about, followed by a few months of pretense, and then an even quicker divorce.

"But you two might hate each other," my mom adds unhappily.

"So what? That's how most marriages end up anyway."

My mother looks totally dismayed and my father hangs his head.

I stand up. "I guess I'd better arrange a meeting with Ashley Winters and – how did Grandpa put it again? Ah yes – use my natural charm on her."

Then I leave the room before anyone has the chance to try and argue with me, or talk me out of my decision. Not that anyone could.

2

FINN

I've seen some pictures of Ashley when she was younger. Long, chestnut brown hair, glasses, bad skin, and chubby cheeks. I also had a private investigator do a bit of digging into who she is. He found out she'd turned her back on the corporate world and dedicates herself to running a charity that helps get homeless kids off the streets, but I can't believe she works here.

To say the area is run down would be an understatement. I hardly dare to leave the car. Partly, because I'm expecting to be mugged the second I get out, and partly because I suspect my car will be gone when I get back outside.

Ok, so I'm exaggerating a little bit, but this place has bad vibes written all over it.

I was expecting... I don't know... something that at least looked inviting. The place is anything but inviting. It's a one story building nestled between a grubby looking greasy spoon and a boarded-up newsagent. It hardly screams 'I know how to make money work for the people I'm trying to help.'

I check the address on the text Andrew sent me one more time, sure I must have the wrong place, despite the faded sign hanging over the entranceway telling me I'm exactly where I'm supposed to be. The address checks out, as I knew it would. I sigh to myself and get out of the car. As the car locks engage and the red alarm light flicks on, I look around me warily. I'm trying my best not to be judgmental, but it's hard when my car is probably worth more than some of the buildings around here.

Maybe my grandpa wanted me to marry this girl because he felt sorry for her, stuck working in a shithole like this. God, couldn't he have just left her some money? She could certainly use the money, and my chances of reaching an agreement with her were getting better with every passing minute.

I think it would be easier to get donations if her charity was based somewhere slightly more flashy.

I imagine my grandpa watching me, laughing at my discomfort, taunting me from beyond the grave. The thought of him enjoying my discomfort forces me inside the building.

The lobby is tiny, but thank God, it's nicer inside the building than outside. Everything still screams cheap though. The chairs for visitors to wait on don't match each other and the table placed next to the chairs is far too low for the height of the chairs. But I have to admit it also looks scrupulously clean and tidy. Even the floor is shiny. And the air smells of freshly brewed coffee, always a good sign in my book. A large vase of artificial flowers stands at one end of the reception desk.

Behind the desk is a woman who looks to be in her early twenties, pretty with curly blonde hair and perfectly applied makeup. She's wearing a tight fitting black polka dot top. She looks up and flashes me a friendly smile.

I feel a spark of hope. If this girl's attitude is anything to go by, maybe Ashley will be easier to persuade than I'm thinking. I flash back a smile and move towards the desk. "Hi," I say. "I'm looking for Ashley Winters." I wait for the girl to smile again, maybe even blush a little, as she tells me I've found her.

Instead, she nods curtly towards her left. "Down the hallway, third door on your left," she huffs sourly.

Oh well, looks like Ashley is not popular with her. I start down the only hallway I can see. It occurs to me that this is part of my grandpa's plan. Ashley is probably one of those hippy types who doesn't shave her armpits and refuses to shower until there's world peace or some shit like that. My grandfather always seemed to want to throw me into the worst situation. He thought it was good for character building, but he wouldn't choose anyone too far outside what he considered feminine and socially acceptable.

Or would he?

My grandfather had always been interested in making money, lots of it, not the scene that went with it. It was my mom's side of the family who'd been interested in impressing society. Grandpa was self-made and he instilled a sensible work ethic in my dad and a furious one in me. I think he picked me to succeed him a long time ago. My mom was old money, more interested in how she was perceived than anything else. Maybe my grandpa who never got on with her has chosen a tree hugger type just to horrify her.

I guess I'm about to find out because I've reached the third door on the left. The hallway is far from fancy. There's no carpet, just ugly, cracked floor tiles. The walls are painted a disturbingly bright white. Let me put it this way. If there'd been the smell of boiled cabbage in the air, I'd be hard pushed not to imagine it belongs in a third-rate hospital or a prison. But I guess if you're homeless, then this would seem like heaven.

The door to Ashley's office is ajar and I tap on it, then step into the tiny room. It has a threadbare brown carpet and the same brilliant white walls. They must have gotten the paint cheap in a job lot or something. Not only on Ashley's desk but all around her on the floor is stacked with files and papers and I honestly cringe at the sight of it. I'm a minimal-ist. I hate mess and excess. How can she work in that kind of chaos?

She is on the phone and waves me towards the lone chair opposite her.

I take a moment to study her.

She is twenty-seven, but she looks more like a teenage boy. Petite, thin, seemingly flat chested and around five foot three at a guess. NOT my type at all. I'm a simple man, I go for chesty, blonde girls with mile-long legs. Ashley looks so thin I imagine a good hard fucking would break her in half, something I tend to avoid in women. I don't want to take a woman to bed only to have to hold back in case I hurt her. Anyway, we won't be fucking so that's a relief.

Also, her dark brown hair is in what I think is called a pixie cut. I instantly hate it. The style is unflattering and not in the least bit feminine. Admittedly, some women can pull off short hair. Unfortunately for Ashley, she's not one of them.

I take in her face. She has lost her glasses which is a good thing. She has full red lips and warm brown eyes, and granted, she's not completely unattractive, but would it kill her to wear a bit of makeup? It's like she has no interest in how she presents herself to the outside world, which for me, is a major turn off.

She's wearing a blouse that looks a little bit too big for her, and I know without even having to look that she will be wearing shapeless trousers and sensible shoes. Maybe she thinks by trying to look masculine, people will see past her small, delicate frame and think she's a force to be reckoned with. However, with the way she has started yelling into the phone, I don't think she needs to dress like that to be taken seriously.

"Just get it done," she snaps and hangs up the phone.

I move to the chair she had indicated and pick up a stack of papers from it. I look around for somewhere to put them, but of course, there is nowhere. Giving up on finding any empty space, I sit down and put the papers on my lap.

She looks at me properly for the first time since I came into her office. If she recognizes me, she doesn't let on. She smiles, and her eyes light up, making her look almost radiant.

Okay, so maybe she's not totally masculine.

"I swear the red tape in this country gets more ridiculous every day," she condemns. "It's like the government wants kids to feel hopeless. Anyway, what can I do for you?"

"I'm here to fix your computer," I say.

"Excuse me?" Ashley asks, with a slight frown. "I think you might have the wrong building. Our computers are fine."

"They work properly?" I quiz.

She nods.

"Ah! I gave you the benefit of the doubt and assumed they were broken when you ignored all of my emails. I guess you're just rude."

"I'm rude?" Ashley snaps. "I think you'll find it's considered rude to barge into someone's office then sit and check them out like they were a piece of meat hanging in a butcher's shop."

I can't help it, the words trip out of me, before I can hold them back, "Oh honey, you wish."

She blushes bright red, and clears her throat. "Actually, I wish you'd just leave. I can't believe Rachel let you in here with that dumb story."

I assume Rachel is blondie. "I didn't tell her that story," I say. "I just asked for your office."

Ashley rolls her eyes with irritation. Obviously, there's no love lost there. "So, I assume you're here to tell me what your emails say rather than just moan about me ignoring them? Although, I must warn you, if I ignored your emails, they obviously weren't interesting enough for me to want to respond to them, so you're probably not going to like my response."

I grin charmingly. "And here I was thinking you were just playing hard to get."

She frowns darkly.

I get to the point, "I emailed you to invite you to lunch."

"*That* was you?" Ashley asks, her frown deepening ominously. "The charming email demanding I present myself at some pretentious restaurant to discuss a mutual interest?"

Clearly, she's using the word charming sarcastically, but I decide to play along. She's easy to fluster, and it's turning out to be kind of fun watching her become more and more incredulous. If she doesn't watch it, she might pop right in front of me. "I'm glad you thought it was charming. Personally, in hindsight, I think it was a little arrogant, but now we're back to you being rude. You clearly got my email and ignored it. Even if you didn't want lunch, would it have been so hard to send back a quick 'no, thank you'?" I pause.

Well, she doesn't disappoint. She blushes bright red. Another reason she should make the effort and wear a little makeup, her emotions are too easy to read. "Of course, I ignored it," she huffs. "I don't take well to being ordered around by anyone, least of all a total stranger."

"I'm not a total stranger, but that's not the point. You do realize now that because of your stubbornness, we're going to have to eat lunch in this neighborhood, a place I can only describe as unsavory."

She laughs then, a confident, gorgeous laugh. "Oh honey, if you scare that easily, then I was right to ignore your email."

This catches me by surprise. I expected her to maybe take offense at my observation, but I thought she would try to defend her choice of getting an office in the middle of a slum. Instead, she's judging me. Someone with that haircut judging me is just—well, wrong. Something about this girl just rubs me the wrong way. From the moment I laid eyes on her, I've been doing and saying things I would never normally dream of saying to a girl. "I didn't say I was scared. I just don't fancy eating somewhere where the cleanest guests are probably the rats in the kitchen," I shoot back.

I know I've gone too far when Ashley's face clouds with real anger.

"Get out of my office," she shouts.

I've come this far, I might as well keep going now. I shake my head and smile.

"It wasn't a request," she adds. "Get out and don't come back here. Oh, and by the way, you're far too old for that preppy schoolboy outfit."

Despite myself, I can't help but glance down at my khaki slacks and shirt. It's neither preppy, nor school boy. "I'm not about to take fashion advice from someone who looks like she dumpster dives for her clothes."

"Oh, you're one of *them*," Ashley leers, nodding to herself.

She doesn't elaborate, and although I know I am playing right into her hands, I have to ask, "One of what?"

"One of *them* who will wear anything with a designer label. Because if Ralph Lauren or Gucci tells them it's acceptable, then it must be. I think the word for that is clone," she finishes with great satisfaction.

I don't know whether to be angry that she thinks I actually have no style of my own, or impressed because she is so feisty.

Before I decide, she smiles sweetly at me. "This meeting is over. Have a good day." She flips open a file sitting in front of her, dismissing me. Very likely, she has no idea which file it even is.

It's a dismissal tactic I've used several times myself over the years, but I'm not one to be dismissed. "So you're not interested in hearing about the proposition I have for you?" I ask coolly.

Ashley glances up from the file and shakes her head. "Nope. I have zero interest in anything you have to say."

I shrug my shoulders and stand up. "It always strikes me as a shame when people running charities let their emotions get in the way of what could amount to a sizable donation of sorts, but never mind. There are plenty of charities who could use the money."

"Wait," Ashley calls as I turn away.

I turn back, one eyebrow raised.

She swallows hard and tries to smile. "Donation? I guess I could spare five minutes."

Just then, something odd happens inside me. I want to make it hard for her. I want to see her beg me to rip her ugly skirt off, open her legs, and fuck her hard on her desk. *Jesus!* Where the fuck did that come from? The stress must have gotten to me. I am literally going insane. Slightly disorientated by the unwanted images inside my head, I sit back down. I rub the back of my neck to compose myself, then meet her eyes. "I told you earlier I'm not a total stranger, and that's true." I extend my hand over the desk.

Ashley takes it, eyeing me somewhat warily.

"I'm Finn Jagger, Arthur Jagger's grandson."

Her eyes widen slightly as she releases my hand.

I go on, "And you're the granddaughter of Walter Winters, my grandfather's business partner, correct?"

Startled and confused, she nods. "Yes, but I haven't spoken to my family in years. Not since I decided I didn't want to marry a monkey in a suit."

I shift uncomfortably in my chair. This is going to be even harder than I thought.

"It's funny," she carries on, "how I was the golden child of my family until I decided I wanted to do something worthwhile with my life," she admits, bitterly. She catches herself revealing too much, and gives her head a little shake.

I decide to gloss over the moment and try to take away a little of her discomfort. "It's okay. Some people just aren't cut out to marry into the corporate world. It's hard. It takes a tough woman to put her needs after her family," I say.

Her face clouds again.

I realize I've said the wrong thing again, although it was unintentional this time. I was actually trying to sympathize with her because I wouldn't want to give up my precious time to care for others either.

"You sound just like my grandfather. He didn't get it either."

"Get what?" I ask.

"That this isn't easier," she replies.

Before I can even open my mouth to reply she goes into a passionate rant, "You think it's hard to be married to some rich guy? Then try sitting here with a fifteen-year old boy who has run away from his abusive father and been on the streets for six months. Try making that kid, who has been shat on by everyone in his life who was meant to help him, trust you. Try making that kid see that you're not like the rest of them. That you're not going to throw him away like trash. Try making that poor kid see his worth. Then you'll know how hard this choice is compared to being the pampered wife of a rich man."

I swallow hard, uncomfortable suddenly. Ashley is turning out to be someone very different from who I thought she would be. "I-I couldn't do that," I say honestly.

She raises an eyebrow, waiting for the punchline.

I shake my head. "I'm serious, Ashley. I talk in facts and figures. I wouldn't know where to start with a kid like that."

She sizes me up for a moment, and she must see that I'm not patronizing her because she relaxes slightly. "So what? You looked my charity up and decided to appease some of your corporate guilt by throwing money my way?" She pauses and smiles, a genuine smile. "Not that I'm above easing your guilt in that way."

I find myself returning her genuine smile. "It's a little bit more complicated than that. It seems that somewhere along the way, before your grandfather sold his shares to mine, they decided we would be good together."

Ashley frowns.

I rush on before she can interrupt and close me down completely. Like what I would have done if someone came to me with that ridiculous story, "My grandpa passed away a couple of weeks ago and ..."

"I'm really sorry for your loss," Ashley murmurs.

I nod and go on quickly, "I'm here about a clause in his will. To get his shares in his company, a company I have spent the last three years of my life pouring everything I have into, I have to marry you."

Ashley stares at me for a few seconds then throws her head back and laughs.

It's not the reaction I'm expecting at all, so I just sit here in silence, watching her for a moment.

She sees the way I'm watching her and the laughter dies in her throat. "Oh, my God, you're serious, aren't you?" She asks incredulously.

I nod grimly.

She shakes her head at me. "This is just typical of my grandfather. He dangles a bit of money in front of you and expects you to sell your soul for it."

"Marrying wouldn't exactly be selling your soul."

"Wouldn't it?" She asks archly.

"Maybe it wasn't your grandfather. Maybe my grandpa thought you could change me, make me do something good with my life. Join you in the charity business." Even as I say it, I know it's not true. I don't know exactly what he wants to achieve except make my life awkward, but he definitely wouldn't want me to sell out and go into the nonprofit sector. I know what he thought of those guys.

"You really believe that?" Ashley asks, her head tilted to one side.

I shake my head.

She smiles again. "Good. Then you're not as stupid as I thought. I still don't know why you're here though. Are you thinking that giving some sort of a donation will be a way of getting the last laugh over your grandpa?"

I shake my head slowly, trying to work out how to word this.

Ashley's jaw drops. "What? You're actually considering marrying a complete stranger to get his company!" She gapes at me like I'm crazy.

Maybe I am, this might just be the most insane idea I have ever considered.

Her jaw drops even further. "And you're thinking I might consider it too. Fucking hell, is this a... proposal?"

"I am considering it," I say cautiously. "But it's not a proposal in the way you think it is. It'll be a business arrangement. I would donate a huge, very huge initial sum of money to the charity, then we'll draw up some sort of contract so the charity gets a percentage of the profits each month. We can really make this work for both of us."

She's still staring at me like I'm insane. "God, Finn. Are you hearing yourself? This... this arrangement of yours is completely, utterly, and totally preposterous. Let me save you some time. Don't bother working out any details, or drawing up any contracts, and certainly don't even think about buying a tux, or roping in a best man. There is no way in hell I'm letting my grandfather map out my future for me in this way. The answer is never."

"Hang on—"

"There are no buts or hang ons with this one," Ashley cuts me off. "This is a firm no for me. I don't care how much money is in it for me the answer is no. No. No!"

I hold up my hand. "I can see that you are feeling very emotional about this. But remember your life need not change in the slightest bit. The only change will be a marriage certificate, which you can put away in a dark cupboard and forget about. You don't even need to see me. After a very short while, we can initiate divorce proceedings. Think how many of those fifteen year boys you can save with all that money."

She takes a deep breath. "I don't want to sound horrible or

anything, but let me make this crystal clear for you. I would rather be buried alive than marry someone like you."

"I dread to think what you would have said if you were trying to be horrible." Weirdly, I'm kind of impressed she didn't lay down for the money. I don't know a single woman who would have said no to me and my extremely generous proposal.

I stand. Not because I've given up, but because I know I need a different strategy.

"Believe it or not Ashley, the idea of being married to someone as stubborn as you isn't exactly my dream either. But I can see the benefit of it for both of us." I fish into my pocket and pull out one of my business cards. "Here is my card. Just in case you decide to start putting the charity before your own personal prejudices."

I hold the card out.

She takes it and looks at it.

For a second, I think she might be starting to reconsider the idea.

Ashley looks over it and then she drops it into the waste paper basket. "Goodbye, Finn."

3

FINN

I run on my treadmill, faster than a jog, but slower than an all-out sprint. My gaze is turned toward the window. From this high up, I feel almost as if I'm flying. Except for the fact, my lungs are burning and the muscles in my legs are aching, which ruins the illusion. But even so.

My favorite time to work out is early evening in the winter with the rain lashing down outside, and lightning forking through the sky. It's a far cry from this workout. It's mid-afternoon and the sun is shining. I'm feeling restless and frustrated, running almost always gets me focused, at least it used to.

My main problem right now is Ashley Winters and her flat out refusal to even consider my proposal. For the record, I realize I fucked up. I should have taken my grandpa's advice and been charming. Instead, I was cocky, arrogant, and made it sound like our marriage was a done deal. I suppose in my mind it was.

It never really occurred to me that Ashley might say no to such a plum deal. I didn't expect her to take one look at me then fall in lust with me like the stupid fantasy I indulged in, but I did expect someone with a business mind who runs a seriously underfunded charity to see the sense of the deal I offered. Maybe I should have mentioned how short a short-term arrangement it would be. Only as long as it took for all of the paperwork to go through and we could probably be divorced within six months. Also, I should have made it even clearer that it would be nothing more than a business arrangement and she wouldn't be curtailed in any way at all.

I guess none of it matters now.

I fucked up in good style, and no matter how hard I try, I can't think how I can approach her again. I can't arrive with a box of chocolates and flowers because she would see right through that. I've already played the *think how many fifteen year old boys you could help with the money*. Maybe, if I had told her just how much was at stake... I know instinctively though, I could offer her a billion and it would make no difference.

In fact, I've got her so riled up I can't even imagine her agreeing to see me again, let alone changing her mind about the deal. I know I should inform Andrew Garfield that the marriage won't be happening, but I haven't yet. It's only been a day since I spoke to Ashley, and I'm still clutching at straws, still trying to convince myself I can turn this around.

Who knows, maybe I can. Maybe some idea will come to me over the rest of the weekend. It had better. I didn't take the whole weekend off to feel this restless energy, to hear this irritating little voice in my head mocking me for failing so spectacularly.

I took the whole weekend off, something I never do, to come up with some genius plan to convince Ashley this is a good idea. There's still time. It's only Saturday. Maybe I'll feel more inspired tomorrow.

One thing I know for sure... running isn't clearing my mind or bringing new ideas. If anything, it's making me feel even more hopeless. Even the music I have pounding through the room isn't distracting me from my negative thoughts. With a sigh, I reach out and turn the speed of the treadmill down to start my cool down. I think maybe I should lift some weights. If nothing else, it might get rid of this tight ball of frustration inside of me.

I coast through my cool down, until my slow jog becomes a walk, then I turn it off and jump off. I pick up a towel and rub away the sweaty sheen that's formed on my skin. I drape the towel around my shoulders as I move towards the first rack of weights. Just as I'm about to pick one up, my intercom buzzes.

I'm not expecting anyone and I frown. I shrug and turn the music off, heading for the intercom. I press the talk button. "Yeah," I say.

"Hi, Mr. Jagger. It's Matthew from the front desk. You have a guest that isn't on the approved guest list."

"Who is it?"

"Ashley Winters," Matthew voices, almost apologetically.

Well, well. I feel the surge of wild victory. Like a caveman who finds out a hot woman is standing at the mouth of his cave. Pity, she doesn't have the hairstyle to make the image work. "Thanks, Matthew. Send her up, please."

I look down at my sweat soaked shorts. I don't have time to change fully, but I slip them off and pull on a pair of grey sweat pants hanging on a rail.

I move out of the room and through to the living room, the towel still draped around my neck as I wait for Ashley to arrive. The bell sounds as I get to the door. I open it and there she is.

She's wearing a pair of blue, high-waisted jeans with a lilac t-shirt. On her feet is a pair of brilliant white sneakers tied up into two large, neat bows. God, her fashion sense is fucking tragic.

She doesn't speak when I first answer the door. Instead, she just looks at me, her eyes moving down my body, taking in the fact that I am shirtless.

I think I see a slight stain of color begin on her cheeks, but I can't be sure.

She catches herself staring at my chest, clears her throat primly, and quickly shoots her gaze upwards until she is looking me in the eye. "I shouldn't have come here." She lets her eyes stray down to my chest again before looking back up at my face, a look of judgement passing across her features. "And you're clearly entertaining."

"If that were the case, I guarantee you that I wouldn't have stopped to see you," I explain. "I was working out."

"Oh," she mumbles, and this time, she does blush. A deep red. Not unattractive, though.

Great. If this were a match. *Finn, one, Ashley, zero.* I smile politely. "Why don't you come in and make yourself comfortable while I go and change into something a little more appropriate." I step back and open the door all the way.

She nods once and steps inside. Her eyes are all over the place as she takes in the living room area. It's a massive open plan room, cavernous and airy. The kitchen stands at one end with a mini bar beside it and a dining area set up. The black leather couch and chairs are positioned to give the best view of the city. Ashley doesn't speak, she just stands mutely looking around.

"Make yourself at home," I say. "I won't be long."

I move across the living room, down the hallway and into my bedroom. I quickly throw on a pair of black ripped jeans and a white t-shirt. I run my hands through my hair, getting it back into some sort of style. I glance at myself in the full-length mirror. To my surprise, my eyes are glittering with excitement. I frown at myself.

What the actual fuck, Finn?

This is just an arrangement.

I move back to the living room, and for a second, I think Ashley has changed her mind and left. As I move further into the space, I see her standing on the balcony, her arms resting on the railing.

Her back is to me as she looks out over the city. She must

have sensed my eyes on her, because she turns around. She looks awkward as she steps back into the room. "I'm sorry. I just wanted some air," she trails off, looking down at her too white sneakers.

"It's fine. I told you to make yourself comfortable, remember." I shrug. "So, what brings you here, Ashley?"

She looks up at me and her expression changes. Gone is the flustered woman who stood before me a second ago, replaced by someone with purpose. "I did a bit of research into you after you left my office yesterday."

"Really? Isn't that like cyber stalking or something?"

"It was when you did it too," she points out.

Ashley, one, Finn, one. I nod for her to go on.

"I have a question. Why is someone like you, who was born into money and never wanted for a thing in his life, so desperate to get his hands on his grandfather's company that he would even consider this insulting arrangement?"

I shrug. "I have my reasons."

"Yeah, I figured. What are they?" She presses.

"I want what should be mine."

"Bullshit," she retorts. "You wouldn't go to this much trouble just for the money. You don't need it. So that makes this personal."

"Okay, you got me. It's personal. My grandpa set me a final challenge and I intend to rise to it."

"We're getting warmer, but that's still not the full story, is it?

If you want me to even consider this, then I need to know the truth."

"You want the truth? Here it is. My grandpa was a hard man to work for and he might have driven me crazy at times, but he also gave me a chance to prove myself. He expected a lot from me, but he pushed me and believed in me in a way my parents never really had. My parents just expected me to take a fancy title in a prestigious Fortune 500 company and bring in cash without killing myself in the process. As a matter of fact, I can do that right now. Simply stay on as CEO at the company and earn a whopping salary and do little to earn it.

She stares at me unblinking.

"But my grandpa knew I would never take that option. I'm doing this because despite what you might think, I care about this company. It was his whole life and ever since I joined it, it has become mine too. I refuse to sit back and watch his life's work go down the shitter because the board is too short-sighted to see that things need to change if we are to keep the company viable in today's market. Is that honest enough for you?"

"Yes," Ashley agrees simply.

I am angry suddenly. Not at her, but at myself for revealing so much. I don't know how Ashley got me to do it. I would never have admitted any of this, even to the people I've known all of my life, and yet here I am, pouring out my truth to a complete stranger. One I'm not sure I like. "Now it's my turn to ask you something. Why are you so against this idea? I did look into you, and I know your charity is barely staying afloat. The donations you receive barely cover the admin costs and you're not able to help even a quarter of the amount of people you'd like to. So what is stopping you from accepting my offer? And please don't say it's just your own stubborn pride. That would be too... too sad."

"You don't know me. Don't you fucking dare stand there all high and mighty making assumption about why I do, or don't do something!" She snaps.

"I'm not. I asked you for your reasons," I point out.

"Same thing," she begins, then stops, then starts again. "You know what? This isn't worth it." She moves towards the door.

"You *thought* it was worth coming all of this way," I say to her back.

She stops moving, but she doesn't turn around.

I take a deep breath. I can't believe I've fucked it up again. *What is it about this girl that makes me say all the wrong things every fucking time?* "Look, you're here now, why not stay and talk about it? I'll fix you a drink and we can discuss it like two adults. Don't let your emotions cloud your judgement. Think of it logically, like you would think of any business deal." I move towards the mini bar, purposely turning my back on Ashley and not looking at her. She can make her own choice now. She can stay, or she can leave. I want her to stay. I really think I can persuade her to see the logic in this, but I'm not about to beg.

Not yet.

I told her the truth earlier – I don't want to see the company being run into the ground by a load of stuffy old assholes. But I rather not have to beg her for this. Maybe if she'd been a different kind of woman. Anyway, why should I? She will be getting as much out of the arrangement as I will be.

I have no idea what Ashley likes, or whether she even drinks alcohol. For some weird reason I think she might be a Bacardi and Coke girl. I reach for the bottle. She can take it or leave it... if she's still here when I turn back around. My ears are on high alert for the sound of the door opening, which hasn't happened yet, but that doesn't mean she won't bolt at any second.

I make the drinks and turn around.

Ashley has turned back to face me. She holds my gaze in a bold challenge.

I can outstare an owl. I keep her gaze as I approach her and she drops hers after a couple of minutes. She moves towards a couch and sits down. I feel a great relief sweep over me. There's a long way to go here, but the fact she's sticking around means she's at least willing to consider doing this. I hand her one of the glasses.

She takes it, smiling her thanks. "What is it?"

"Bacardi and Coke."

She frowns. "Your report was that detailed?"

"No, I just guessed. You look like a Bacardi and Coke girl."

She studies me suspiciously. Obviously, she doesn't believe me.

I take the couch opposite to hers and watch as she gingerly

sips at her drink, finds it to her liking and takes a longer drink. She looks up, catches me watching her, and surprisingly adorably, looks shy. She puts her drink down on the coffee table and straightens her spine.

"Right," she decides firmly. "Back to business. You asked me earlier why I came here. I came because you're right. The charity is struggling massively, and we've just been turned down for some government funding that would have made a big difference. I would do anything to keep the charity going. The young people we're helping don't need another slap in the face; they don't need to think that one more person who they've come to trust has abandoned them. So that's why I'm here. I'm here to hear you out and consider your offer."

"Good," I say. "I really do believe we can help each other, Ashley. So here's my offer. If you agree to this, you get one hundred thousand dollars right there and then. You'll receive another two hundred and fifty thousand the day after the wedding. And you'll receive one percent of the monthly profits. Obviously, that can fluctuate, but as a rough guide, we made just short of an eighty million dollar profit last year. So you'd be looking at approximately sixty five thousand dollars per month."

"Wow! You have no idea what a difference that would make," Ashley exclaims.

"So you'll do it then?"

"Before I answer that question, I need to ask you something. And I want you to be honest."

"Of course," I say. "Naturally, I don't expect you just to take my word for this. We'll have lawyers draw up a formal agreement, and I'll allow your accountant to see the books and everything."

She smiles at me and shakes her head. "That's not what I meant. The money your company makes, I would trust that you wouldn't try to rip off a charity."

"That's something I would never do. For a monkey in a suit, I'm actually pretty honest."

She smiles and blushes again then she turns serious, although her cheeks only get redder. "What I want to ask you is a little more personal. Finn, do you actually want to marry me?" She asks.

"No," I say immediately. And it's the truth.

"Why not?"

I hesitate. "You sure you want to hear this?"

She nods. "Absolutely, be as blunt as possible."

"Okay, you've asked me to be honest, so I am going to be. You're not my type... at all. You're too little for one thing. I've never ever been with a woman who was as small as you, and I think I'd be afraid I'd hurt you. Plus, your hair is way too short and your dress sense is... well, it's almost like you're going out of your way to repel people. I've never really considered marriage, but if I was going to get married, it would be to someone who wanted to make a home, not rush off to her office before me." I realize I have probably said too much and I rein myself in before I can say anymore. "I guess that's not what you wanted to hear, but you did ask for brutal honesty."

Ashley laughs softly. "I definitely could have done without the list of my faults as you perceive them, but that's actually exactly what I wanted to hear." She smiles at my confused expression. "You're the one who told me to take the emotions out of this, Finn. I just wanted to make sure we're both on the same page, that you're not secretly looking for this to turn into anything."

"Absolutely not," I admit quickly. This was easier than I thought it would be. "And in the interest of equality, why don't you tell me all of the reasons why you wouldn't want to marry me. Assuming there are any of course." I wink at the last part.

Ashley rolls her eyes. "Okay, but remember you asked for this."

I nod. Her insults would be water off a duck's back and it would be good to get it all out in the open.

"Well firstly, you're rude and arrogant, and I can't stand that in a person. You were born with a silver spoon in your mouth, and you have no idea of the difficulties facing people who weren't so lucky. You're basically an entitled brat, and the one time you do decide you're going to do something for a charity, it's not about the charity, it's about you getting what you want. If I ever choose to get married, it will be to a man who cares about more than just himself."

I raise my brows at this assessment.

"Oh," she adds almost like an afterthought. "And you're far too concerned about material things, and what you look like. Although I suppose that comes with the territory of being a pretty boy."

"You think I'm pretty?" I ask, raising an eyebrow.

"That's not a compliment," she clarifies briskly. "Do you have any idea how much of a turn off it is to women?"

"I hate to disillusion you Ashley, but I can say from personal experience that the majority of women would disagree with you there."

"Ugh, you're so gross," she observes haughtily.

"So we've established," I say easily and smile at her. "I think it's fair to say we don't like each other, and in any other circumstances, we'd sooner gouge our own eyes out than date each other."

Ashley nods slowly. "Yeah, I think that about sums it up."

"So in conclusion, Ashley Winters, I fucking hate you, but will you marry me, anyway?" I say with a smile.

Despite herself, Ashley laughs. With her defenses down, and a genuine laugh on her lips, she is... almost attractive.

But her laugh is truly infectious and I find myself laughing with her. I take a drink when I stop laughing and meet her eyes over the rim of the glass. I move the glass away from my mouth and hold her gaze a moment longer.

She looks away first.

"Is that a yes?" I ask when it becomes clear to me she isn't quite ready to agree to this just yet.

She stares at the ground and swallows hard. This is obviously difficult for her to agree to.

"It's really a no-brainer," I say persuasively. "Since there's no risk of either of us falling for the other and getting hurt. It's only for a few months. Six months tops."

She nods slightly.

"I would do anything to save this company, and although I don't know you very well, I think it's a safe assumption that you would do anything to help these kids." I pause.

Ashley nods harder, confirming she would.

"As soon as all of the paperwork goes through turning the company over to me, we'll get a quickie divorce and go our separate ways. The company will be mine and you'll be able to help all the abused kids you want. What do you say?"

"I have a few conditions," Ashley adds, raising her eyes up to me.

I nod at her stiffly, sure she's going to ask for more money. I can probably swing a couple of things around and give her a little more in the beginning, but ultimately, the business is a business, and I can't condone giving her a higher percentage of the takings.

"One," she ticks it off on her thumb, "you don't interfere with my work. You are not buying into the charity in any way that gets any sort of a say in how I run things. You are just a donor."

Wow, it's not about money? "Agreed," I say instantly. "I have my hands full with my own company, but even if I didn't I wouldn't have the first idea where to start with running that kind of charity, anyway. Although, I will say that if you ever need any help with investments or anything like that, I'd be happy to let you talk to our guy."

She nods, but she doesn't accept the offer.

I don't push it.

"Two," she goes on. "I don't expect you to stop seeing other women, but if we're going to be publicly seen to be engaged and then married, you need to be subtle about it. I won't be seen to be one of those women whose man cheats on them and they turn a blind eye to it all."

I hadn't even considered this part of it, but she's right. I wouldn't want to be seen as a lowlife whose wife is cheating on him either, because for this to work, we have to make it look like a real marriage. "Done," I say again. "And that has to work both ways."

"Don't worry, I also have no intention of looking like some sort of slut who sleeps around outside of her marriage," Ashley announces. "I have no objection if you do, I just don't want to be the laughing stock of the city."

I nod. "Got it."

"And finally, number three. We don't drag this out. We get married and divorced as quickly as possible."

"Done," I say again.

Ashley smiles at me and raises her glass.

I raise mine and we clink them together.

"Finn Jagger, I hate you too and I will be honored to be your fake wife." She drains her drink and stands up.

I get to my feet with her and walk her towards the door. "I'll sort the paperwork out for you to go over tomorrow. And I'll call you within the next couple of days to arrange a lunch with my mother so we can start organizing the wedding. I'll give you the first check at lunch too, unless you need it sooner?"

Ashley smiles. "That will be fine." She starts to move away, but then she turns back, a genuinely horrified expression on her face. "Wait, you want me to meet your mother?"

I laugh softly. "Well of course, but don't worry. You don't have to act like we're in love or anything. My mother knows about this."

"Oh, okay." She looks relieved. "I guess I'll wait for your call then." She goes out through the door.

I close it then lean against the wood and smile to myself. "There you go, Grandpa. Ashley Winters and I are getting married."

4

FINN

I look at my watch for the third time. Ashley is late.

I knew I should have gone to pick her up, but she insisted she didn't want me to. She would come to my place and we could go from here together. I couldn't really insist, as she clearly appeared not to want me to know where she lived. I could find out easily enough, but I figured it would be creepy to search out her home address and turn up there, even though that's pretty much what she'd just done to me a couple of days ago.

I try calling Ashley's mobile again, and again, but it goes straight to voicemail. The thought she has changed her mind is ever-present. I feel like launching my own phone across the lobby, but I resist the urge, and shove it back into my pocket.

It had been hard to convince my mom that this was a good idea. To pull off this marriage thing in a way so it won't be obvious it's a sham. My mom isn't taken with the idea, but I guess ultimately, she knows nothing is going to change my mind, so she's going along with it. But if she senses Ashley isn't committed to doing this, she will be a nightmare to deal with, and quite frankly, I don't have time to keep trying to persuade her.

I look down at my watch impatiently.

I'm really glad I told Ashley to be here an hour earlier than she actually needed to be. It gives us a bit of leeway, but if she's much later, then we'll still be pushing it.

If there's one thing my mom hates above everything else in a person it's tardiness. I can already picture the pinched look on her face when we get to the restaurant to meet her.

My phone starts to ring and I snatch it out of my pocket, expecting it to be Ashley explaining what the fucking hell she's playing at. Instead, I see Tyson's name on the screen. Tyson is my most trusted assistant, and I asked him to find out where the hell Ashley is. "Hello," I bark into the phone.

"I've found Ashley. You're not going to like this, Finn."

"Don't tell me. She's panicked and booked a flight to Canada or something," I say quietly, a cold claw gripping my insides. She has let me down and everything I've worked for, for so long is slipping away. Even though we both signed that contract, I know I can't hold her to it if she really doesn't want to carry on.

"Worse," he adds. "She got arrested this morning. They're holding her at the police station over on Heather Avenue."

"Oh well, that's just fucking fantastic," I say, and to be honest, it might have sounded like I'm pissed off to anyone listening, but I am wild with joy. She didn't change her mind. Hopefully, she hasn't done anything too extreme and I can bail her out quickly.

I end the call, then phone my mother and tell her something important has come up. I will be late and ask her if we can meet later at her house. She immediately tells me it had been murder to get the booking at that restaurant so she will wait for me no matter how late I am.

I make my way outside, letting the doorman know I'm ready for my car to be brought around. My car arrives in seconds. I thank the valet and get in.

I put the car in gear and pull away, my tires screeching. I'm going to have to get her something to wear first too. Whatever she's wearing is going to be wrong for the occasion, but I assume there's no way in hell she's going to want to go and meet my mother in clothes she's been wearing in a jail cell.

I head towards a small boutique I know. I've taken some girlfriends shopping there and the owner is a friend.

As I step inside, one of the assistants approaches me. "Good morning, Mr. Jagger. Can I help you find anything today?" she asks, with a welcoming smile.

"Yes, actually you can," I say. "I need a dress for my fiancée." It feels bizarre referring to Ashley as my fiancée, but I guess I'm going to have to get used to that. "Something elegant. Something you'd wear to meet your new mother-in-law," I add.

"Ok." The assistant nods. "And what dress size is she?"

I have no idea, so I look the assistant up and down. "She's about two inches shorter than you, but about the same build."

"Ok." The assistant smiles, obviously used to clueless men trying to buy things for their women. "Do you have a picture of her?"

I don't obviously. I pull out my phone. I open up Google, type in Ashley Winters, add the name of her charity, and get thousands of results. One of the hits is a full-length photo of Ashley wearing a white lacy dress. Remarkably, she looks like she's actually made an effort for a change. No doubt, someone else must have dressed her that day.

I show the assistant the photo.

She nods and tells me to take a seat. Within a few minutes, she's back, holding on to a pretty black dress. The dress has long sleeves and a demure neckline. The skirt part flows out from the waist and will probably sit just above Ashley's knee.

It's perfect and I nod. "That's great, thank you," I say, standing up.

"I also picked these out which I think would go really well with the dress," the assistant adds, showing me a pair of nude high heels.

I know it's just a sales technique to try to upsell something, but almost immediately, I am filled with a strange excitement. I want to see Ashley wearing the dress and the sexy pair of shoes. I don't allow myself to think too hard about why I want to see her in these shoes. I just nod again as I take both the dress and the shoes. She puts it onto my account and I rush back to my car and head towards Heather Avenue.

I park my car and hurry inside. "Hi," I say to the desk Sergeant. "I was told I would find Ashley Winters here."

He taps on a keyboard, then looks back up at me. "Yeah, she's here."

"I've come to bail her out."

He nods at me and his eyes are twinkling. "Is she yours?"

I raise my brows. "I guess so."

"A bit of a handful, isn't she?" He remarks with a chuckle.

"For sure," I agree, and allow myself to chuckle with him. "What did she do?"

"She was arrested for trespassing. She was in some fancy office causing a scene. To be honest, she wouldn't have been arrested at all if she had just left when we showed up, but she wouldn't leave, so we had no real choice."

I sigh. I hardly know Ashley, but this sounds like exactly something she would do. I hand the officer my debit card.

He runs the payment then addresses me, "Take a seat. She'll be released in a while."

I know better than to ask him to hurry it up, so I sit down, tapping my foot in irritation. *God grandpa, did you know the girl is a wild cat?* I bet he knew. I just bet he did.

After a few minutes that feels like a few hours, a door opens and the officer steps through followed by Ashley.

Her face falls when she sees me and she turns to the cop. "Oh God, Officer, please just take me back to the cells," she mocks, rolling her eyes. "The last thing I need right now is another corporate suit."

The officer gives me a look I can read easily enough. *Good luck.*

Yeah, I'm starting to think I'm going to need it. "Let's go," I say to Ashley, my voice is tight.

She follows me out of the station, but once we reach my car, she refuses to get in. "Look Finn, the last thing I need right now is a lecture from you, okay." She turns to walk away.

I grab her wrist. "I just paid your bail to get you out of there and I damn well expect an explanation."

She rolls her eyes. "Let's just say the slimeball I was confronting is lucky I couldn't get to him. If I could have, then I would have been arrested for something a lot more serious than trespassing. But his office was locked and I couldn't get in. The door was pretty solid actually. But I guess a guy like that needs something solid to protect him."

"For fuck sake Ashley, you knew we were having lunch with my mom today. How could you be so damned childish and irresponsible today of all days? Couldn't your little one woman crusade against the machine have waited until tomorrow?"

"Actually, he threw his sixteen year old daughter onto the streets because he found a little bit of pot in her room. By the time we found her, she had been raped," Ashley mourns. "So no, it couldn't have waited until tomorrow. And if your mom doesn't get that, then quite honestly, I don't think I want to meet her. In fact, this just proves that we're too different to make this work, even for a few months. Why don't we just call the whole thing off?"

Her first words take the wind out of my sails completely and I feel my anger drain away, replaced with something altogether different. In fact, no, it isn't all that different. It's still anger, a deep burning anger, but it isn't focused on Ashley. It is focused on the bastard who thought throwing a kid onto the streets was okay. Anger for the girl whose life had been ruined because of a shitty father who had let his temper get the better of him.

Before I know what I'm doing, I find myself wrapping my arms around Ashley.

She goes stiff in my arms for a moment, then she sags against me and lets me hold her.

"Hell, Ashley, I'm so sorry," I mutter. "I had no idea."

Suddenly, she pushes away from me, back in control of herself again. "No, you didn't. And that's what I mean, Finn. We're just too different to do this."

"No, we're not," I argue. "Our passions lay in different places, but we both feel that fire. We can do this. We are doing this, Ashley. You've already signed the contract, and I'll fucking carry you over my shoulder down the aisle if I have to. We can reschedule today, but that's it."

She exhales heavily.

"Don't you want to have the resources to help more girls like the one from this morning?" I ask.

She gets the message loud and clear. If she doesn't do this, she won't have the resources to help people like that girl. "Alright. Let's just get it over with," she finishes sullenly, then gets in the car.

I slide in too and pull away before she changes her mind. I check my watch. "We're meeting my mom for tea instead. We have about half-an-hour."

She leans back against the seat and closes her eyes.

"What were you planning on doing if the door hadn't been locked?" I ask Ashley, glancing over at her in the passenger seat.

"I don't know." She shrugs. "I didn't think about what I was doing, I just heard that girl's story and I snapped."

"You could have gotten hurt," I say.

"Not as hurt as she is," she replies, turning to look at me.

"What happens now?" I ask.

"Nothing," she replies. "He'll drop any charges, because if he doesn't, then the reason I was there comes out. Don't worry though, I'll pay you back the bail money."

I wave away her offer. "Don't worry about it. Call it my good deed for the day. Speaking of which, the first check is in the glove compartment."

Ashley opens the glove compartment and takes it out. She

runs her fingers over it, then she promptly pushes it into her hand bag.

"You need to change," I say. "And there's no time to go to your place. I picked something up for you. You'll have to change in the car."

"No way." She shakes her head. She's saying it before I even finish my sentence. "If you think I'm clambering around in here changing, then you're very much mistaken."

"It's a dress, Ashley. It really won't be that hard," I say.

"Ok, then let me rephrase it. I'm not getting changed in front of you," she snaps.

"Really, you can. You have absolutely no worries about your body turning me on." I thought to put her at ease, but I see instantly it has the opposite effect.

She turns towards me, her face full of thunder. "I think we've established that you don't find me attractive. And I can do without you reminding me of that fact every two minutes. I'm not changing in front of you because I have a bit of self-respect, not because I'm assuming you won't be able to keep your hands off me."

"I just meant..." I start then I sigh. "Oh, forget it. I'll find a service station somewhere and you can go into the restroom there."

"You know what Finn? I'm perfectly comfortable how I am," she asserts. "Just drive to your mother's place."

I subtly look at her out of the corner of my eye. She's wearing black trousers which aren't too bad, although they aren't the best fit. Her blouse is a problem though. It is shapeless and very crumpled. And her shoes. My God, her shoes. They look like something a grandmother would consider the height of fashion, sensible, flat black lace ups complete with her signature ridiculously big bow. To be honest, right now, I don't care if she is dressed in a sack, but I know my mom will care. A bad first impression with my mom lasts a lifetime.

I know if I point out that her outfit is hideous, it will only make her dig her heels in so I try a different approach. "My mother will be dressed up and you are her guest. You'll feel out of place," I say.

"Don't sit there and try to tell me how I'll feel," she snaps. "I've told you I feel perfectly comfortable how I am. Why don't you just be honest and admit you'll be ashamed of me."

"I'm not."

"Then you have nothing to worry about. Your mom knows we're not really together. And anyone else seeing us together will never dream we are *actually* together. They'll probably think I'm some random employee you've taken pity on and brought along."

That's exactly what they'll think, but I'm not worried about them. What I'm really worried about is the fact that my mom will take one look at Ashley and write her off as a bad idea. She won't take the time to get to know Ashley and find out that beneath the awful clothes and the seemingly endless anger, there's actually someone under there who has a good heart. Why, I want her to like Ashley is a mystery to me. I've never cared one way or another what my mother thought of all my other girlfriends. "Fine Ashley, have it your way. Let my mom see that you're not in the least bit invested in actually making this thing work. That you're just in it for the money."

Again, she surprises me.

She doesn't take the bait at all. Instead, she laughs at me. "Finn, that's exactly what I'm in this for. And you were right earlier; we have a contract now, one neither of us can back out of. There's no dress code in the contract, so you're just going to have to accept that I am who I am, and that I'm not going to dress up like some airhead debutant to impress your mother."

I give up. I sit there, quietly fuming and Ashley does the same. Let her go in there looking like this, I think to myself. Let her show herself up and regret it. I'm honestly past caring about whether or not this is awkward for her. I might even tell my mother the true reason we're late. See how she fucking likes that. Because my mom won't care that she was doing something noble and brave. All she'll see is a girl who has no idea about how commitments work and how, when you make an arrangement with someone, you keep it or let them know in good time that you won't be able to make it.

By the time we arrive at the restaurant, we're almost half an hour late for lunch and the icy atmosphere between us is so cold I almost expect to see her breath steaming in front of her face.

We get out of the car, still not talking to each other, barely looking at each other, and Ashley slams my car door so hard that I grit my teeth.

The valet hurries forward to take my keys, and I walk into the restaurant, figuring Ashley will either catch up with me or she won't. "Booking under Jagger," I say to the smiling host.

"Yes, Sir," he says, looking down to consult the book he has open on his small lectern.

Ashley has joined me now and she stands by my side. The host doesn't show any change of expression when he glances at her, but I know that's only because he's trained not to. I glance at Ashley out of the side of my eye.

She's looking around, taking in the modern décor and the tables where people in designer gear are sitting chatting and laughing. But most of all, she's taking in how totally out of place she is in this setting. She glances down at herself and then back up. "Is it too late to change?" she hisses at me.

"Ah, there we are, sir," the host announces. "The rest of your party is already here. Follow me please." He is already walking away.

"It's fine." Ashley sighs. "It's my own fault for being so stubborn."

I know I can't make this right now. There's no way to get her back out of the restaurant without my mom spotting us through the window, especially now as the host is almost at our table. My mom's favorite table is the one right by the window and I know she's probably already seen us coming in.

"Don't worry," I say to Ashley with a wink. "You'll do great."

I find that I no longer want to punish her for being so stubborn. She's obviously managed that herself, and she's done it way harsher than I ever could have.

My mom stands up when she sees us approaching. Expressionlessly, she looks Ashley up and down, but she makes no comment about her disheveled appearance.

"Nice of you to join me," my mom says, when the host has moved out of earshot.

"Hi, Mom," I say kissing her cheek. "I'm so sorry we're late. I got caught up with a client and I didn't realize the time. By the time I was finished, we didn't even have time to pop to Ashley's place, so she could change. She's been doing some decorating for me in one of the offices."

My mom's expression changes instantly when she thinks Ashley is only dressed this way because of me. She clicks her tongue at me and gives Ashley a sympathetic smile. "I'm sorry about my son and his workaholic tendencies. Would you be more comfortable if I asked for a table somewhere a little more private?"

"Oh no, honestly it's fine," Ashley reassures with a warm smile.

"Alright, dear." My mom smiles back. "I'm Helen by the way, as it seems my son has forgotten his manners completely." She leans forward and kisses Ashley's cheek.

"And you probably already know that I'm Ashley," Ashley informs as she sits down.

My mom picks up her menu. "I guess we better order."

Ashley catches my eye while my mom is distracted, *"Thank you,"* she mouths.

I don't know why this makes me happy, but it kind of does. I decide not to question why I'm happy, but instead, just be grateful that I am.

5

ASHLEY

Mrs. Jagger, well, she asked me to call her Helen, looks at me as though I'm out of my depth and even Finn is starting to feel sorry enough for me that he covered for me. But I'm not out of my depth. I could fit in here if I wanted to. Hell, I used to fit into places like this just fine. I just choose not to anymore. Five years ago, this place would have been one of my local haunts, but I'm not that person anymore.

Five years ago, I was just like Finn; a cog in the glittering world of the moneyed, ruled by wanting to win at all costs. I still want to win, but now at least, I'm fighting for something worth fighting for. When I win now, it's not about screwing over the little guy or making millions of dollars. It's about changing someone's life, giving them a fresh start when they need it the most.

The day I left the corporate world behind, I left behind all of its trappings. I stopped buying clothes that cost enough money for a family to live for a week. I stopped driving a car that cost more than some people's homes. And as I shed the materialistic stuff, I realized I didn't miss any of it at all. In fact, I found the very notion I had once been one of those desk monkeys abhorrent. Looking back now, it's like I'm looking back on someone else's life rather than my own.

My parents weren't happy about my decision to go into the nonprofit sector, but they got used to the idea, and I think now, they're just happy I'm happy. Or at least my dad pretends to because my mom wants to keep the peace. My friends were a different story. My friends were a group of Finns and when I left that life behind, we all realized just how little we had in common. The only thing tying us together was a life I was no longer living. It's not like they weren't supportive, it's just that they didn't get it and I no longer got them. I kind of drifted away from them, and the odd time I run into one of them now, we're civil enough, but it's like we're strangers. I suppose in some ways we are.

I am much happier now, living a simple life and helping people, but holy shit... I wish I'd put the stupid dress on now. I'd expected Helen to be one of those executive type women who wear sharp suits and snap at everyone, trying to prove they're every bit as strong as their male counterparts. I've taken down plenty of those types over the years, and I knew in my mind exactly how to handle Helen.

The trouble with this plan is Helen isn't corporate. I can see this by looking at her. She's wearing a neat white blouse and a black skirt. Her collar is open showing a string of pearls. Her slightly greying hair is rolled into a chic chignon and her earrings match her necklace. Everything about her screams upper class. She is more like royalty than a part of the corporate world.

And I have no idea how to handle her.

Although she has been warm to me, I can tell she doesn't approve of any of this, and I can tell she doesn't approve of me. Generally, when I meet people who are so openly judgmental of me, I cut them out of my life, but I'm kind of stuck with Helen for the near future. If I were dressed more appropriately for this place, for this lifestyle, I would have had some armor at least.

I would have been back in my old clothes, playing my old role. The role where I fit in with the Helens of the world. The role where she would have been pleased to think her son was marrying me. And it wouldn't have mattered that it was all fake.

A waiter comes over to our table.

Helen gathers up the menus and hands them to him with a cool smile that declares I'm being polite because I'm civilized, but you're not important.

I wonder how the waiter feels. He probably doesn't even notice it anymore as most of the clientele in here probably look at him the same way. I bite my lip to stop myself from smiling as I imagine the waiter in a bar or something after work with his friends talking about taking crap from these people and saying how clueless they are as to how the world really works.

We order our meal.

"And bring a bottle of your finest champagne," Helen orders

in a clipped accent she probably thinks makes her sound classy, but just makes her sound pretentious, as far as I am concerned.

No one speaks like this naturally. I can't help but think if a person is truly comfortable with who they are, they don't need to fake things to make themselves feel more important than they actually are. I decide to stop being a bitch. Helen is clearly old money, and she's probably never known anything different to this lifestyle. It's no more her fault she was born rich and blinkered than it is when someone is born poor and sees too much too young.

"Yes ma'am." The waiter nods, and scurries back away, fading into the background just like he's been trained to do.

Helen turns to me. "I hope you don't mind me being blunt, dear."

I shake my head. I actually don't mind. I like honesty, even if it hurts, and I would prefer her to get the objections and the accusations out of the way right off the bat.

"I am not a huge fan of Finn going through with my father-in-law's ridiculous request, but he's explained his reasoning to me, and I will support his decision. I understand why he's doing it, and I understand why you're doing it. I can't say I understand Arthur's reasoning, but he was an old fool. Anyway, my point is that we all know this is nothing but a sham marriage, and I just want to make it clear to you now that you will not receive a penny more than what the agreement states. Are we clear?"

"Jesus, Mom…" Finn starts, his voice hard.

I've never heard him speak like this before, but I interrupt him, "I can fight my own battles, Finn."

He turns to stare at me.

I look him square in the eye. Something flashes in his eye and I can see he is not happy to back down. "Please?" I implore quietly.

His adam's apple jerks, then he nods curtly.

I turn to Helen and almost tell her the truth; that I have a background in contract law and there is at least one loophole in the paperwork Finn sent over which I could exploit if I really wanted to. I won't, because I have no intention of whoring myself out for my own personal gain, but I could. Instead, I decide to tell her a version of that part. "I have no problem with that, Helen. I'm not sure what sort of women you associate with, but let me assure you that I am not for sale. I am going along with this agreement only because the money will help so many people who truly need it. I don't need your son's money to make my life better and I have no intention of trying to get a penny more than what our contract stipulates."

Unembarrassed, she nods with satisfaction. "I'm glad we're all on the same page here. Now, let's get down to the actual wedding."

I snort out a laugh which I manage to turn into a fake cough. The very idea of planning a fake wedding just strikes me as funny. I mean what's to plan? We'll go down to the Justice of the Peace office one afternoon, sign some papers and it's done.

It seems Helen has other ideas though. She leans down to the ground and pulls a huge binder from a leather bag.

I look over at Finn.

"Totally up to you," he offers with a shrug.

Helen puts the binder on the table and opens it. "I'm just going to run through some of the details, but don't worry too much about taking it all in right now. Damon will go through everything with you in more detail later."

"Damon?" I ask.

"Damon Brown," she repeats and looks at me like she's waiting for me to magically know who he is. When it's clear that isn't going to happen, she shows the first sign of discomfort. "He's the best wedding planner in the city, and he's agreed to do this for me as a personal favor. The wedding will be in one month and you have a lot to decide."

I'm still trying to get my head around the idea that we need a wedding planner when Helen opens the binder and begins pointing to things and giving me a running commentary of the contents.

I peer down at the images in a daze. *Wow! She has been planning this for a very, very long time.*

"Locations. You can choose from a cathedral wedding or a location wedding. We would be more than happy to host the wedding at our house, which I think would be a nice touch as it's Finn's childhood home. Or of course, there's Melbourne Hall."

I definitely don't want to get married in a cathedral, or

somewhere as fancy as Melbourne Hall. I get the impression Helen wants me to choose her home anyway, but it feels wrong. If Finn gets married there, it should be to someone he has a future with.

Helen doesn't wait for me to offer up any comment before she flicks over the page. "I've scheduled you an appointment at a bridal boutique so you can choose your dress and of course your bridesmaid's dresses. How many would you like? I think four is appropriate as Finn will be having four groomsmen."

"Helen, may I say something?"

"Of course." She looks at me expectantly.

"Well, it's just... isn't this all a bit elaborate for a fake wedding?"

"Young lady, I am going along with this to make Finn happy, so he can have what he wants. That doesn't mean I am going to allow the two of you to make a mockery of me among my friends. Which means your wedding will be every bit as grand as it would be if this was all real." She pauses, her face scornful. "Do you have a problem with that?"

I have a million problems with it, but I find that I don't want to voice them. I'm doing this for the kids. Finn is doing it for his company. And she is doing it to keep her status.

Slowly, I shake my head.

"Good."

"Who will pay for all this?" I ask, biting my bottom lip. There's no way I will be asking my parents to chip in.

"Is that what you're worried about?" She sniffs. "You can stop worrying. I made my expectations clear in terms of what you will and won't get from my son, but I don't expect your family to pay for this wedding. I appreciate that it's me insisting on this, so it's anything other than a quickie Justice of the Peace job as Finn so charmingly put it. So please, just enjoy being a fairytale bride and let me take care of the finances."

I open my mouth, not sure what I'm even supposed to say to this. I hope she's not expecting me to thank her, but I have a horrible feeling that's exactly what she's expecting.

The waiter saves me from saying the wrong thing as he appears with a bottle of champagne in a silver bucket. He pops it open and pours our glasses.

Once he is gone, she raises her glass towards both Finn and I. "To all our happiness."

I smile and so does Finn.

For a moment, we are all connected in a lie we have been forced into. We all take a sip. Then Helen turns to Finn. "You don't mind, Finn, if I talk to Ashley for a bit, do you?"

"Be my guest," he invites putting the glass down.

Helen turns back to me, the awkwardness from before the waiter arrived seemingly forgotten and launches back into her folder. "Your cake will be made by Anton's Bakery, one of the nicest in the city. He's made wedding cakes for royalty, you know. You will have a meeting with him to choose your flavors and decorations. Perhaps nothing too modern though, huh? Think elegant dear – less is always more." Her eyes slip down along my legs to my shoes.

Ah, the bows. She doesn't like the bows. *Tough. I like them.*

I nod in agreement. She has a very clear idea in her mind of how she wants this wedding to go. It is at the tip of my tongue to suggest she do whatever she wants and lets me know where I have to be and when, but I resist the urge. I kind of get the impression she genuinely believes she's being nice doing this, and while I can't quite get my head around that, I don't want to throw her kindness back in her face.

She pushes her book of weddings towards me.

I flick through the pages. It has options for catering, options for reception venues, suit hire, flowers, wedding favors, centerpieces, bands, officiants, witnesses, vows and poetry for the ceremony, and a hundred other things that just leave my head spinning.

I feel grateful when the first course has arrived.

"Bon appétit," she coos, before delicately slipping between her pale lips the smallest piece of *foie gras* I have ever seen.

As she carries on speaking two things become certain. Firstly, this wedding is easily going to cost in excess of half a million dollars, and secondly, I was wrong earlier. I am well and truly out of my depth here, and I will be no matter what I'm wearing.

When Helen finishes talking, I pick up my glass and realize it is empty. I have drunk the entire contents of the glass without even tasting it. More for something to do with my hands than anything else. I put the empty glass back down.

Helen smiles at me, warmth in her eyes for the first time. "Don't worry, Ashley. I know I've fired a lot of information at you, but like I said, Damon will go over everything properly with you later. He has a copy of this file, and he knows what choices are pre-approved. I would prefer you stick to those options, but if there's something you want that isn't mentioned, have Damon run it by me alright?"

I nod mutely, as our main courses are served.

"Now, how many people will you be inviting?" Helen asks briskly.

No one, I want to say. I mean the whole thing is a sham. It's not something I want to share with anyone. I hate the idea of being that girl who has a big fancy wedding and then gets divorced a few months later. Besides, this a far cry from the quick wedding Finn had talked about.

"Surely, you must want to invite your family and friends," she prods.

Actually, I don't, but if my friends and family find out I had a wedding and didn't invite them, they would probably never speak to me again. I do a quick calculation in my head. I'll have to invite my parents obviously. Aunt Shauna, Uncle Jim and their daughters. And the people I work with. I cut into my mushroom main course and a gorgeous golden sauce made of butter oozes out. "Around twenty."

Helen laughs, then she catches herself when I frown. "Oh, goodness me, you're serious," she utters, shocked.

"Yes. I don't have a big family and I've always imagined a small, intimate ceremony if I ever did get married, with only my closest friends around. I understand this isn't going to be that, but I really don't want to invite all of my acquaintances. You can invite whoever you want, obviously, but I'd really prefer to only invite people I actually like for my guests."

"If you're sure that's what you want, dear," Helen concedes. "I've already ordered the stationery. If you can send Finn a list of names and addresses by the end of the day, that would be great. The announcement will be going out tomorrow, and people will expect their invites shortly after."

This means I would have to tell my parents sooner rather than later. It didn't so much matter about my friends. None of them were the kind of people who would read anything that carried society wedding announcements, that much was for sure. "Okay," I agree, my mind blank.

"Just a couple more things, Ashley. I trust that you will use your discretion and not breathe a word to anyone of this being anything but a real marriage between two people who love each other," Helen pontificates.

I nod quickly. "Of course," I agree. I don't add what I'm thinking. Why Helen might be worried about what society would think of her, and I really don't get that, but I do get why the news of our fake wedding getting out would be bad. I don't want people whispering about me, talking about the girl who married for money, even if it is for a charity rather than for herself. If anything, I am more determined to keep this whole thing under wraps than Helen. The hardest part of this for me is going to be convincing my friends that Finn is different from how he appears. How beneath his cocky swagger, and all his flashy money, he's a genuinely nice guy that I could fall in love with.

Whoa! Where did that come from? I could NEVER EVER fall for him. NEVER.

"Good," Helen says decisively. "And... of course, I expect you to throw yourself into planning this wedding. If you have an appointment, I expect you to be there. And please don't allow Finn here to make you late for everything. If you think there's a risk of that, call me and I will arrange a car to come and collect you. And Ashley, our family has a certain reputation to uphold. You won't dangle out any skeletons for anyone to pick up on, will you?"

Wow, what would she think if she knew I had come here straight after being arrested? Maybe I should tell her and call this whole thing off. I am seriously debating doing just that, but then I see the faces of the kids I would be helping, and the faces of the hundreds of kids we would have to turn away due to a lack of resources, and I know I can't risk this not happening. "I'm an open book Helen. There are no skeletons in my closet," I say as my plate is cleared away.

Helen is all smiles now. She has gotten her way. "Do you have any questions, Ashley?" She really has pulled off a big coup.

How did I just agree to be the bride in a sham wedding that's going to be almost as big as the royal wedding of Harry and Meghan? "No," I say, sneaking a look at Finn.

He is watching me with a look of amusement.

I look away quickly. "I think it's all clear. Or at least it will be when I get a chance to wrap my head around it all."

"Oh, you'll do fine," she reassures me. "Now, I have to run. Ashley dear, promise me you'll at least try to enjoy all of this."

I smile and nod, although I think Helen and I have very different ideas of fun if she thinks this is something I would enjoy.

She puts the folder back away, collects the leather bag and her red crocodile skin Birkin, then she stands up.

Finn stands with her and I quickly follow suit.

She air-kisses my cheek, does the same to Finn, orders him to call her later, then she's gone, leaving behind nothing but a faint cloud of her expensive perfume.

I am starting to understand Finn a little more now, growing up with her as a mother. It's clear she loves him and wants him to be happy, but from the little I've seen, it appears she's one of those parents who showers their children with money and material things rather than hugs and kisses. I can understand why Finn thinks so highly of his grandpa, who it seemed, didn't let him get away with any shit. The man must be the one who showed him that money means nothing unless you've earned it yourself through hard work.

I try to remember why I'm mad at Finn. Oh yes, he said my body was unattractive. And he hates my hair. And he thinks I have no dress sense... I would do well to remember that.

"Wow!" I breathe out a heavy breath of relief. "That was intense to say the least."

Finn grins. "If you thought that was bad, you don't want to see her when someone pisses her off. Believe it or not, she actually seemed to like you."

He has a nice smile. It makes his blue eyes sparkle and look warmer. It's a shame he's such an asshole behind the smile. I remind myself that we are not really friends. We're just natural enemies who have been thrown together by his grandfather for reasons unknown.

"Ooooh... remind me not be around when she's pissed off." I laugh nervously. "What made you think she liked me? The part where she presumed I would try to rip you off, the part where she assumed my family couldn't afford such a wedding, or the part where she warned me off showing your family up by bringing one of my skeletons out of the closet?"

Finn's eyes positively twinkle. "All of the above."

"I have to give her a credit though. She clearly knows people. After all, I have just been arrested and I could be again. And my family couldn't afford this wedding. In fact, hardly anyone I know could afford this wedding. Finn, don't you think this is an awful lot of money to throw away on something that's not even real?"

"It is, but it's her money and it makes her happy. I'm just glad she's finally come around to the idea that I'm going to do this."

"But think of all the good she could do with that money instead. I could put her in touch with several charities that would take her hand out for even a tenth of what this wedding would cost, and surely even in her exalted circles something like that would be well received."

Finn's lips twist. "Yeah, I know exactly what she would say to that idea. It's not that she wouldn't want to give any money to charity. She actually makes a lot of donations. It's just that no matter how much she donated, she'd still do the wedding this way. If it makes you uncomfortable, I can say something to her. Would you like me to?"

I can't help but laugh at that suggestion. "Are you joking? Seriously Finn, I would rather cut off my own arm than piss her off."

Finn laughs too.

It's nice to see him laugh. We have spent so much time bickering and trying to outdo each other in the insult stakes that I realize it's only about the third time I've heard him laugh. He should do it more often. It is great to see he has a good sense of humor beneath the prickly sarcasm.

"Bullshit," Finn scoffs. "You were willing to kick down an office door and confront a guy who doesn't even care if his own daughter got hurt this morning."

"Yes, and I'd do that again tomorrow. Trust me, he wouldn't have been half as scary as I imagine your mom would be if you told her I didn't approve of any of her wedding plans."

"You could be right there. The best thing you can do here is just go with the flow. Choose the lesser of two evils at every turn," Finn suggests.

I nod. It seems like that's about my only choice at this point.

"How do you feel about some dessert?" He asks.

I want to, but I shake my head. "No, thank you. I'm not really hungry to be honest."

"Really? I saw you salivating as they went back with the dessert trolley," he teases. "I know we're never going to be best friends or anything, but we're stuck with each other for the foreseeable future now, so we might as well at least attempt to be civil to each other."

"It's not that," I mumble, looking down at the table, not able to meet Finn's eye.

"Then what is it?" He asks.

I look back up and feel the heat flooding my cheeks as I do. "You were right. I feel completely out of place here and I really don't want to hang around any longer than I have to."

"Got it," Finn says, standing up abruptly.

Great. Now I've pissed him off. The one time I wasn't even trying to. "Finn..." I start.

He turns back and grins at me.

I feel relief flood through me to see he's not pissed at all.

"This place is hardly me either, Ashley. Let's go grab a burger and maybe some pancakes," he suggests. "I know a great place downtown."

I feel myself smiling as I nod. "Now, you're talking."

6

FINN

The drive to the pancake joint is a lot more relaxed than the drive to the restaurant was. In some ways, I think meeting my mom has subdued Ashley a little, but in other ways, I think it's actually made her like me a little bit more.

By the time we're sitting down, eating pancakes dripping with maple syrup and loaded with whipped cream, fruit, and nuts— we haven't insulted each other once. This has to be a record. It's been at least half-an-hour. Maybe she can see now that I'm not half as bad as she thinks.

"Do you realize something, Finn?" she asks, grinning at me over her glass of diet Coke. "In this place, you're the one who's totally out of place. You're so overdressed in your designer suit." Her eyes are twinkling.

I know she's joking and I find myself grinning, instead of snapping back. I shrug. "You're right, but this is who I am, and if people don't like it, they're perfectly welcome not to look. And really, if the people here have nothing to talk about other than my clothes, I feel sorry for them."

"You thought the people in the restaurant would judge me for what I was wearing," Ashley points out.

"Oh, I knew they would. Because I know they have sad little lives where criticizing someone wearing the wrong clothes or picking up the wrong fork at the dinner table is the most interesting topic of gossip they can possibly think of."

"You know, sometimes it sounds like you have such contempt for the world you live in," Ashley observes.

I frown.

She shakes her head and smiles. "That was a compliment Finn."

It's my mother's world and I don't actually hold it in contempt, but I guess to her, it is a compliment so I just smile back and let it go. I like this Ashley and I don't want to go back to arguing. "So you worked in a law firm?" I ask, changing the subject.

"Yeah," she tells me. "I was a contract lawyer. I spent my days finding loopholes, so rich guys could screw over poor guys."

"Sounds fun," I comment.

"It was and it wasn't. I hated what I was doing to small businesses and everyday people." She pauses, "But I must admit I enjoyed the intricacy of the work. Scouring five hundred pages to find the one word that changes the whole meaning of the document. When I left that world, I actually debated doing something similar, only on the side of the little guy."

"Why didn't you?" I ask. "I know what you're doing now is probably more rewarding, but why did you give up something you love?"

"When I really thought about it, I knew I just couldn't do it. I knew it would be too heartbreaking. I admire anyone who puts themselves on the line like that day in and day out while knowing they will lose ninety-five percent of their cases. I know all of the corporate tricks because I've used them all. Do you have any idea how many unwinnable cases I won because I dragged the case out with continuances, and swamped the guys with thousands of pieces of paperwork, knowing they didn't have the resources to cope with it? It was just a waiting game until the little guy ran out of money and lost his lawyer and then the case was over. I couldn't bear to be on the other side of that."

"Counter suing was my grandpa's favorite tactic. They sue you. You sue them back for twice the amount they're suing you for."

"This is exactly what I am talking about," Ashley hypothesizes. "It is so infrequent that the small guy wins. At least now, I'm not the one dangling a thread of hope to someone I know has none."

I grin. "And you think I'm included on your bad corporate monster list?"

"Yes," Ashley agrees immediately.

"Why exactly do you think I'm only interested in screwing people over?"

"You sell computer software, right?"

I look at her curiously. "Yeah."

"I've seen the profit margins. I know how much the company rips people off."

"Not anymore if I have my way," I say. "That's the big change that I've brought in that the board disapproves of. I convinced my grandpa that people want this software, but they want it at affordable prices. I showed him a business model where we could sell the same product for half of the price and still make as much profit because it will become more widely available to the average consumer."

Ashley raises an eyebrow at this.

I smile and feel almost proud that I've impressed her. I shake my head slightly. *What the actual fuck? Since when did I start caring what Ashley thinks of me?*

"That's actually pretty admirable." She smiles, a twinkle in her eyes again. "And I'm just going to gloss over the part where you're still making the same amount of money."

"Ah, but look at it this way," I remark. "If the profits had taken a hit, then my grandpa never would have agreed to this. And even if he had, what do you think would have happened? Layoffs, that's what would have happened. And believe it or not, I don't want to be responsible for half our staff losing their jobs. No matter what you think, I'm not a monster who doesn't give a shit about anyone but myself."

"I never said that," Ashley shoots back defensively.

"You didn't have to."

"Maybe we both misjudged each other a little bit," Ashley concedes.

"Yeah, I think maybe we did."

"Why do you think your grandfather put this marriage to me clause into his will?"

I have pretty much given up on trying to figure out what my grandpa's motives were with this one. I think I'm just going to stick with the notion he set me a final challenge, one he didn't think I'd rise to. I wonder if he's regretting that now, because the more I get to know Ashley, the more I don't think this is going to be so unbearable.

"Earth to Finn," Ashley mocks, pulling me out of my head.

"Sorry. The truth is, I don't really know. He wasn't the sentimental old fool that my mother thinks he was. Even to the very end, he was the sharpest pencil in the box. He must have known I would try to buy my way out of it, maybe he just wanted to give some money to a good cause in his will without looking like a sap."

"Well, in that case, I have an idea if you're not busy this afternoon."

I think about the pile of paperwork on my desk, the ton of calls I still have to make to close a deal I'm working on. I really am busy this afternoon, but I'm also incredibly and irresistibly intrigued as to what her idea is. "I could spare a few hours."

"Great." She smiles. "Let's go then. I thought maybe you'd want to see where some of your money is going to go."

"Sure," I agree as I drop some money on the table and we get up. "Where are we going? Back to your office?"

"Nope."

She's wearing a smile that tells me I'm not going to like what comes next.

"I'm going down to the soup kitchen to hand out meals to some homeless kids. We can always use an extra pair of hands."

This isn't what I thought I was signing up for, but I don't want to see disappointment cloud Ashley's face. Suddenly, I *want* Ashley to like me. I have never particularly cared one way or the other if people like me or not, and I wouldn't have given a shit if someone like Ashley judged me, but now, I don't know what's happened, but yeah, I really want to make her happy.

"Lead the way," I say, and to my surprise, I'm actually looking forward to being the extra hands next to Ashley in the soup kitchen.

7

FINN

By the time Ashley and I leave the soup kitchen, I have had my eyes well and truly opened. I mean, don't get me wrong, I knew we had homeless people in the city, but honestly, I've never really stopped to think about their plight in any great detail. For the most part, I think they brought it on themselves by choosing not to work.

Like so many other people, I chose not to see them. Of course, I've thrown bits of change into their outstretched hands before, but I've never really stopped to think about what it must be really like to live on the streets. I've never stopped to think about what it must be like to be constantly cold and hungry, to be constantly shunned and avoided.

I've never thought about the dangers facing these kids every day either. Or what it must be like to be hungry and thirsty, then see people who seem like they have everything, throwing away a half-eaten sandwich. But even more poignantly, I've never considered what it must be like to have nothing and no one in this world, to feel like you don't matter, like no one cares one way or the other about whether you live or die.

It's a sobering thought and some of the stories I've heard today made my hair stand on end, and others made me burn with anger. After a couple of hours, I started to understand why Ashley does what she does. It's not about self-gratification, it's about hearing these stories and realizing that if you just stand back and nod sympathetically, then you are a part of the problem.

I made a decision while I was there. Even if Ashley backs out of this deal, she's still getting the money. Obviously, I won't be able to give her so much each month because that will be out of my hands if the board takes over the company, but she'll still get the lump sum, and if I walk away from the company and start my own, then her charity will get a percentage of that.

I'm not about to tell her this though. I might have had my eyes opened to the lives these kids are forced to lead, but I haven't gone completely soft in the head. I don't want to give her an easy way out, which would mean I lose everything.

"You surprised me in there, Finn," Ashley murmurs as we get into my car. "I kind of expected you to keep the kids at arm's length."

"Honestly, I surprised myself," I admit. "I didn't expect to find myself hugging kids and listening to their stories either." I turn slightly to face her. "And I definitely didn't expect to feel like this."

"Feel what?"

"To feel... as if I did something important," I admit honestly. If I had gone back and tackled my to-do-list it would have been satisfying, but it would never have felt like this.

"You didn't expect it to feel rewarding?" Ashley asks, with an eyebrow raised.

"No," I say softly, but suddenly, I can't look into her searching eyes. What I'm feeling is too real and too hard to articulate. I turn my gaze back to the front, put the car into gear, and pull away. "Are you going home now?"

"No. To the office, please."

I nod and turn the car in that direction.

For a while, there is silence. Then I let it pour out, "I didn't expect to feel so angry about what was happening to these kids. I didn't expect to feel so protective of them." I can feel Ashley's eyes on me, but I don't turn to look at her, instead I keep my eyes firmly on the road, even though we're at a red light.

"You expected them all to be druggies or rebellious, didn't you?" Ashely asks. "Kids you could tell yourself brought their misfortune on themselves." Her voice doesn't sound judgmental. It sounds resigned, like she experiences it every day.

"Yeah, I did," I confess. "And I know why. It's easier to ignore the problem and tell yourself it's not up to you to fix it if you let yourself believe that the homeless are not your problem. That they somehow, don't deserve their situation exactly, but that they're somehow responsible for their own mess.

But when you see how many of them are just kids, then you can't pretend anymore."

"For what it's worth, I thought that way myself once too." Ashley nods. "Until I started working with these kids, that is. That's why I fight so hard for them, because aside from all the obvious challenges they face, people don't realize how much prejudice they face. Can you imagine Finn, being fifteen and not having eaten for three days? And every adult that passes you by just shrugs it off, and doesn't help you. Imagine how that must feel."

"I don't want to imagine it," I say quietly.

"No one does, because then they know they'd be forced to act.' Her voice changes slightly.

I do look at her then, just a quick glance.

She's smiling. "But you know the difference between you and ninety-nine percent of the people in this city who are in a position to help? You are helping. The money you are donating is going to make a huge difference to these kids' lives. But more than that, you sucked it up, went in there and actually helped them. You spoke to them like they mattered, and while there are still people willing to do that, then these kids still have hopes and dreams for a better future."

"I don't know about that," I say. Her words of praise are doing things to me.

"Well I do." Ashley laughs then. "And I have to say I was quite impressed that you didn't throw a fit when you ended up with gravy down the front of your shirt," she adds.

I glance down at myself and I can't help, but smile. There

are spots of gravy, spots of some kind of tomato based sauce and who knows what else caked onto my shirt. I'm not the only one who came out of there to help serve the food, but I'm probably the only one who was dumb enough to refuse an apron.

"It's only a shirt," I say. "Plenty more where this came from."

Ashley makes a disapproving noise and although she's still smiling, the spark has gone from her eyes.

Once again, it is clear we are from different sides of the fence. For a while, I climbed the fence and went to her side, but now I am back where I belong.

We ride the rest of the way to her office in silence and when I drop her off, she flashes me a quick smile, then disappears into her office building.

8

FINN

I look at my watch when the doorbell sounds. It's almost midnight. I groan internally. It's probably going to be one of my buddies, drunk and avoiding his wife. I stand up when the insistent ringing comes again. I've got too much on my plate to be listening to the drunken raving of anyone tonight. Normally, I'd be willing to help out a friend, but I have an important international three-way meeting scheduled for twelve-thirty and it won't do to have a drunk prancing around in the background.

To my total astonishment, I see Ashley through the peephole. I pull the door open. "Umm, hi."

"Hi," she greets brightly, but she doesn't offer any explanation as to why she's here.

"What brings you here so late?" I ask.

She sighs then, a heartfelt sigh that makes her smile slip from her face, and allows her distress to show for a moment. I don't know what's happening, but she's clearly not one of my drunk friends and I'm not about to send her away. I step back and gesture for her to come inside. As she steps past me, I see a large duffel bag slung over her shoulder.

"I came by a couple of times earlier, but you weren't home," she says as though that explains everything.

"I was working late."

"I see I made the approved visitor list," she remarks, with a half-smile.

"Well, you are going to be my wife. It would be a little weird if you didn't."

"About that, Finn," she starts.

"There's no changing your mind now, Ashley. You know as well as I do that it's too late for that. You've already met the wedding planner and things are moving."

"I'm not backing out. I just... do you have a minute?" She asks.

I subtly check my watch. It's just about twelve. I can spare a little time.

"I'm sorry, I know it's late," Ashley rushes on.

Obviously, I wasn't as subtle as I thought I was with the watch. "It's fine. Sit down."

Ashley puts her large bag down on the ground by the end of the couch and sits down.

I sit down on the opposite side.

We're both in the same spots we were in the last time she turned up here and we agreed to this deal.

I look at Ashley, waiting for her to explain what's going on.

"The lease ran out on my apartment a couple of months ago, and I didn't get it renewed. It's seriously hard to find a decent apartment anywhere in this city unless you have thousands of dollars to spend on rent each month, which I just don't. I moved back in with my parents until I found somewhere suitable. My father and I got into a big argument earlier and well..."

"Okay." I try to sound interested. Doesn't she have girlfriends she can go to with this stuff? I really have no idea what to say to her.

She gestures to the bag. "It ended up with me leaving."

The irony of this isn't lost on me. Ashley, the champion of the homeless, almost found herself living amongst them. "You seem to make a lot of problems for yourself by thinking with your emotions instead of your head," I stupidly blurt out. And that's why she should have gone to someone else for wine and sympathy. It's really not my area of expertise.

Ashley ignores me and carries on as though I haven't spoken, "And it was only when I walked out that I realized I had nowhere else to go. I thought seeing as we're about to be married, and we're going to have to make a show of living together anyway, that maybe I could crash here for a couple of nights?"

Well, that was an easy one. "Sure, why not. Plenty of room here."

"What's the catch?" Ashley asks, even as relief floods her face.

I frown. "What do you mean?"

"You agreed to this awfully easily," she points out.

"There isn't a catch. As you pointed out, we're going to be married soon. How would it look if you were crashing on someone's couch instead of being here? And it's not like you're going to get wasted every night and smash my apartment up. Right?"

"Right." She grins. "I only do shit like that on Thursdays."

She surprises me with her quick humor and I laugh.

She laughs with me.

"I'm hardly ever home anyway, so you'll mostly have the place to yourself, but when I am home and I'm working, I expect you to stay out of the way and not disturb me," I add. I swear it's like a disease. The second I start to feel at ease with Ashley I say something idiotic to remind her why she doesn't like me.

Thank God, she doesn't take my words too seriously. "I think I can manage that," Ashley pipes up with a big smile.

"Good," I say. "Let's put that to the test then, shall we? I have a video conference in fifteen minutes and I don't expect to hear you banging around or anything in the background."

"Got it." Ashley nods. "But seriously. You have a work thing at this time?"

"The client is in a different time zone," I explain. "And getting his business could be a real pivotal moment for us. It's worth working late for." I stand up before she can start asking a ton of questions. "I'll give you the tour." I smile.

Ashley stands up beside me.

I wonder if I should grab her bag. She picks the bag up herself and my moment to look like a gentleman is lost. Oh, well. I figure it's a little late to try acting the gentleman with Ashley now, anyway. She'll probably think I have an ulterior motive and we'd end up in a fight about it.

I point behind me. "So obviously, that's the kitchen and dining area. Like I said I'm hardly ever home, and when I am, I don't relish cooking. I don't keep food in the house for that reason, but if you're ever hungry, look in the top drawer and you'll find a bunch of menus. I have accounts at each of those places. Feel free to order whatever you want."

"You have no food at all in the house?" Ashley asks.

I shake my head. "Nope."

"You're weird."

"And you're very judgmental for someone who has nowhere else to go," I point out with a grin.

"Fair point." She laughs. "I take it back. It's completely normal to have a state of the art kitchen and use it to store take-out menus."

"Exactly." I hide my smile and lead Ashley through a door

and into a hallway. "That's my room," I say, pointing to the first door on the left. "And beside it is my office. I don't expect you'll need to be in either of those rooms. The next door on that side of the hall is a gym which you are welcome to use. The first door on the right is a bathroom which again, you are welcome to use, although obviously, you'll have your own en-suite. That last door on the right is your room."

"And that middle door on the right? Is that the mysterious room I'm not allowed to go in because all of your secrets are in there?" Ashley asks with a wicked gleam in her eyes. "Is that where you keep the bodies of your business rivals who've crossed you?"

"Well, actually it's a linen closet, but I like your version better," I explain with a grin. "Now if you'll excuse me, I really do have to go and get prepared for this meeting. Make yourself at home, okay?"

Ashley nods and she makes her way down the hallway to her room.

I catch myself watching her ass as she walks away and look away quickly before I duck into my office.

ASHLEY

I'm feeling kind of strange as I step into Finn's guest room. I came here because honestly, I have nowhere else to go. Both Mariella and Janice, my two best friends live with their boyfriends and it would be awkward for me to dump myself on them. And anyway, since they got their men, they have had a lot less time for me.

I guess I could have gone to my aunt's house, but I didn't want to have to go through the argument with her and I knew Finn wouldn't care enough to ask me what the argument was about.

The argument with my dad was really just the usual shit. My dad telling me my work is dangerous and me reminding him it's not half as dangerous for me as it is for the kids on the streets. He then went on to point out that's not my problem and as always, it escalated from there. And this time, it didn't stop at its usual place. It turned into a whole bunch of personal insults, and I knew by the end of it that I couldn't stay there.

My aunt wouldn't understand any of it. She'd just tell me to let it go, but it's not that easy. I can't just let it go when my own father thinks my job is worthless. God, I'm such a textbook case. Daddy doesn't love me enough so I choose to work with kids who get no love, so I can feel all warm and fuzzy about myself and maybe find some validation somewhere else.

I shake my head. Where the fuck did that come from? It's almost like Finn is in my head. I shake this thought away too. It's not Finn's voice, it's mine and I just need to get the hell over myself.

Now I'm here... at Finn's apartment, I feel like maybe I've overstepped the mark a little bit. I mean is it normal to turn up at a virtual stranger's home and ask to crash there? But then again, is it normal to come to a stranger's office and ask them to marry you for money? Nothing about the arrangement Finn and I have is exactly conventional.

So...

The more I think about it, the more it actually seems like I'm in the right place. Most people don't wait until after they're married to live together, anyway. Maybe this will help with the ruse, because right now, I still haven't told anyone about the wedding. I just can't figure out how to make the story sound even remotely convincing. I'm just not the kind of girl who meets someone and has the fairy tale romance that ends in a wedding after just a month.

No one who knows me is going to believe that's what happened. I push away my worries; they're the same old worries I've had since I agreed to this and I haven't come up with a solution to them yet, and I don't think I ever will. Instead of worrying, I look around the guest room.

I don't imagine Finn has many guests staying overnight here, at least not the kind that don't share his bed, and yet the guest room is set up perfectly as though he's always expecting an overnight guest.

The bed is a massive king, covered with a soft looking, thick duvet with a pristine white cover on it. The sheets and pillowcases are pure white too. Dang, I'm almost afraid to sit down on it in case I get it dirty. There are bedside cabinets on either side of the bed, a matching wardrobe and chest of drawers. In the corner of the room beside the chest of drawers is a small black leather armchair, positioned to give the best view of the balcony and the city beyond it.

There is so much glass in this apartment that it feels almost like I'm outside. Every room has a stunning view and I spend a moment just standing in the center of the room, looking out over the twinkling lights of the city. I know I should find this kind of lifestyle obscene, but I don't.

I can understand why Finn wants to live somewhere like this. I can understand why anyone would. Searching for an apartment of my own really brought that home to me. I might have lost a lot of the materialistic side of my nature, but I still don't want to live in a shithole apartment, in the sort of place where the hallways smell of urine and people are shooting up on the staircases. Maybe that makes me a hypocrite, but I'm not ashamed of not wanting to live in squalor.

I push my duffel bag off my shoulder and begin to unpack my things. I haven't brought a lot. It wouldn't have been much even if I had brought everything I owned. I hang up my clothes. I have brought three work outfits and two non-work outfits. A handful of underwear, some toiletries, and that's pretty much it.

I wander through to the attached bathroom with my toiletry bag and my jaw drops. This is no little en-suite, although why I thought it would be, I don't know. The room is bigger than my bedroom in my old apartment with a lovely big bathtub and a large shower. It's all cream with fawn accents. I instantly fall in love with how light, bright and airy it looks. I place my toiletries on the marble countertop beside the sink, noting how sad they look in this luxurious room.

I go back to the bedroom and strip off, folding my clothes then laying them on the arm chair. It's only then I realize I haven't brought any pajamas or a night dress. I could sleep naked, but what if I want a glass of water or something in the night and I run into Finn?

I throw my clothes back on with a sigh and head out of the room. I can hear Finn's voice drifting out of his office and I know better than to go to him and ask him if he has something I can wear. Instead, I go to the linen closet, hoping to maybe find something I can wear in there, like a spare robe or something. The closet is filled with towels and sheets, duvet covers and pillowcases. There's even a spare duvet and a bag full of spare pillows.

But there's nothing even remotely resembling a robe.

I curse under my breath and head back towards my room. I guess I'll just have to throw my blouse back on if I need to wander around in the middle of the night. As I reach out my hand to open the door and go back into my room, I remember Finn saying the room opposite mine was a gym which I'm welcome to use. There's not much chance of that. The only time I work out is when I'm so mad I can't quite get rid of all of the pent-up tension inside of myself unless I pound it out on something.

But I'm curious as to what equipment he has so I push the door open and step inside. The room is as well-equipped as any public gym I've ever been to, which granted, is only two, but still. There's a treadmill, a rowing machine, an elliptical, and an exercise bike. And that's just the cardio stuff. There are free weights, various machines I don't even recognize, and a few machines I do. My attention falls on the far wall though. There are a few pegs there and hanging from them is a pair of sweatpants and a nicely ironed, light blue shirt. I smile to myself and grab the shirt.

I'm sure Finn won't mind me wearing it, and it's only for one night. I'll buy a pair of pajamas tomorrow. Even if he does mind, I know he would rather me take the shirt without permission than go into his office while he's having a video conference with a potential new client and ask him if I can wear the shirt.

I go back to my room and strip off down to my panties again. I slip the shirt on. It's big on me, but I like that for bed. It smells of laundry detergent, fresh and clean, which I definitely like. I check my phone and see it's almost one in the morning. I turn the light off and finally slip into bed.

I moan with pleasure as I feel the cool, silky sheets against my skin and the soft mattress beneath me. Finn sure knows how to choose the right mattress and bedding for maximum comfort. If this is the guest bed, I can't help but wonder what his bed is like. I push this thought away quickly before I decide I have to know, and go investigate.

I grin at the thought of Finn's call ending then him going into his bedroom and finding me in his bed, an accidental, dark-haired Goldilocks. I figure I'd be straight back out onto the streets before I could even say *who's been sleeping in my bed*. Wait, no that isn't Goldilocks' line, is it?

Ah well, it's late and that's my excuse for getting it wrong, so I'm sticking to it. I snuggle down into the bed, yawn and close my eyes.

Twenty minutes later, I am still wide-awake and getting more restless by the second. My throat is dry and it's stopping me from sleeping. I sit up and throw the covers back. I slip quietly out of the room and head for the kitchen.

Finn's office door is ajar, light spilling out into the hallway. He's no longer talking so I assume his meeting is done with.

I go to the kitchen, find a glass and fill it with tap water. I drink it down in one go, rinse out the glass, and set it down on the draining board beside the sink. Then I head back towards my room, but I know it's not just thirst keeping me awake. I like to spend half an hour or so before bed losing myself in a good book. No matter how late it is, I seem to need that routine to convince my mind it's time to switch off and sleep. Of course, in my hurry to leave the house before my mom tried to talk me out of leaving, I didn't even think to grab a book.

I wonder if Finn has any.

I give a cursory glance around the living room, but there are no bookshelves anywhere, and the books on his coffee table are those pretentious photobooks meant to send a message rather than be read and enjoyed. I roll my eyes. He's such a walking cliché in some ways.

I go back down the hallway and as I approach Finn's office, I notice the wall I can see through the slightly open door is lined with books. I smile to myself. Surely, there's something in there I can read. Even if it's a business book, it's better than nothing.

I pause in the doorway for a moment, making sure that Finn is definitely not talking anymore. I wait a couple of minutes until I'm confident the meeting is really over and then I tap lightly on the door and step in.

He's sitting behind his desk, engrossed in something he's typing. He glances up as I enter and a frown crosses his face for a second. "Is something wrong?"

"No," I murmur. "I just wanted to borrow a book if that's okay?"

"Why are you wearing my shirt?" he asks, ignoring my request.

"I found it in the gym room and I had forgotten to bring some pajamas. You don't mind, do you? I figured you wouldn't appreciate me bursting into your meeting to ask you."

"It's fine," he replies distractedly. "And yes, you can borrow a book." He goes back to his screen.

I turn and begin browsing the books on his shelves. There are books about every aspect of business, from marketing to sales strategies, from accounting to merchandising. I scan the titles, stepping forward and running my fingers over the spines. None of them particularly appeal to me. I look higher and then I see it. I smile to myself. The top shelf is fiction.

I can't reach the books comfortably, so I no longer finger the spines, but I take them all in. True crime, crime fiction, a bit of science fiction. Thrillers. I spot a Lee Childs book I haven't read yet and I reach for it.

As I reach, I feel the shirt riding up slightly, but I know Finn is engrossed in what he's doing, so I ignore it, and stretch higher.

Finn gives an uncomfortable sounding cough. "What are you doing?" he asks.

This makes me start a little. "You're not very observant for a smart guy, are you?" I quip.

Now I know Finn is watching me, I am conscious of the fact I am almost flashing my panties, and instead of stretching up, I jump up. I miss the book by a fraction of an inch, but I feel air getting beneath the shirt and I feel it billow up slightly as I land. So much for jumping to reveal less of my ass. I feel Finn's presence behind me, so close that he's almost touching me.

He reaches up, grabs the book and practically slams it into my hands. "There," he mutters. "Now, if you don't mind..."

"Oh, I don't." I smile. "You just get back to work and forget I'm even here." I turn away from him and go back to looking at the bookshelf.

"And how am I supposed to do that when you're prancing around here half naked?" Finn asks.

I turn back to Finn, a slight frown on my face that becomes a grin when I realize what's happening here. He got a tiny flash of the lace of my panties when I jumped up, and now, he can't think about anything but my underwear. So much for my body not being able to excite him. "Just remind yourself how repulsive you find my body," I say tartly.

"I didn't say I found you repulsive," Finn replies uncomfortably.

I shrug and grin at him. "No, you didn't use those exact words. And judging by the reaction just now, it seems like maybe you do find my body quite attractive after all."

He doesn't respond.

I decide to tease him a little before I leave. I put the book down on his desk and lift the hem of the shirt ever so slightly. "Does it excite you to see a bit of thigh?" I ask with a little laugh.

Finn frowns.

It's clear I'm irritating him and I know I should just stop and leave, but it's kind of fun watching him squirm, and honestly, at least when he's frowning he doesn't look so pretty. He's actually quite handsome when he frowns, in a brooding, not my type at all kind of a way.

I wiggle my hips, playing with the hem of the shirt. "Have you lost your voice?" I enquire in a fake innocent tone. I turn slowly, still wiggling my hips until my back is to Finn. I peer at him over my shoulder. "How about if I do this?" I lift the shirt up and expose my lacy black panties for a quick second and then I pull it down again. "Oops," I giggle and then I turn back to face Finn.

He looks furious now. "Stop it," he demands, his voice low, almost a growl.

I feel heat flood my body and I blink hard as I notice for the first time how Finn's pecs stand out beneath his shirt. "Or what?" I grin.

"Or I won't be responsible for what happens," he growls.

"Ooh... big talk for a man who's afraid of a flash of thigh," I taunt. I dance back a little and grab the hem of the shirt again. "How about if I lift it right up?" I start to lift the shirt. I have barely gotten it past a few inches when Finn grabs me roughly by the tops of my arms.

"Just stop it, okay? I'm not messing around here, Ashley." He looks me in the eye as he delivers this.

I notice how mesmerizingly hot his eyes are, how I can almost melt into them. Finn is still holding my arms, and I feel my skin tingling beneath his touch. He steps closer to me, still holding my arms and suddenly, our bodies are pressed together. I can feel his cock pressing against me and I am a little shocked to discover it is rock hard. My clit pulses, betraying me. "Why do you want me to stop?" I ask breathlessly. "You were clearly enjoying the show."

He releases my arms, but he doesn't step back and neither do I. I find myself looking into Finn's eyes and neither of us look away. It feels like the room is suddenly charged, full of electricity, and I am shocked when I realize just how badly I want Finn to sweep me up into his arms and kiss me.

My breath is coming in little gasps and I can feel Finn's chest heaving as we maintain eye contact. Usually, when he peers at me this way, I panic and look away, afraid he will be able to read too much in my eyes, but this time, I am determined to hold my ground.

"Jeez Ashley, you're such a fucking child." There's no malice in his voice and I can see the lust clouding his eyes, even as he insults me. "What sort of a woman acts like this?"

The sort who realizes exactly what she wants and is about to get it. "I'm just messing around, Finn. It's called having fun, you should try it sometime. But I guess you're afraid you might fall off your high horse," I say, not taking my eyes off his.

He leans closer to me, so close I can feel his breath tickling my lips when he speaks again, "You're the most irresponsible woman I've ever met," he whispers.

"And you're the most arrogant man I've ever–"

My last word is swallowed up in Finn's mouth as he presses his lips against mine. I feel like I have been unleashed as our lips move together and I press myself more tightly against Finn, pushing my hands into his hair. He wraps his arms around my waist, moaning into my mouth as his hands slip beneath the shirt and caress the skin of my back. Fire floods my body and I can feel my pussy getting soaked as Finn's tongue moves into my mouth, meeting mine.

I pull back slightly from Finn's mouth. "You shouldn't have done that," I pant.

"I know," he agrees.

I lean forward and kiss him again, a light kiss that teases me, that makes my pussy clench, my body ache for his touch. I pull away again. "You definitely shouldn't do it again."

He looks at me for a moment, indecision in his eyes, and then with a moan, he pulls my body against his again. We kiss deeply, hungrily, and our kiss is so intense that it's almost angry.

I reach down blindly and begin to fumble Finn's pants open. My body is screaming at me, desperate to feel him inside of me and I don't want to deny myself this simple pleasure any longer. I try to remind myself that I hate Finn and everything he stands for, but my head isn't in control, my body is, and my body wants this more than it's ever wanted anything before.

I get Finn's pants open, but before I can get them down, Finn pulls away from me. He doesn't speak, he just spins me around. He pulls me backwards, my body colliding with his, my ass against his hard cock. He kisses my neck, nibbling hard enough to make me cry out as sweet, stinging pleasure floods through me.

I put my head back, giving him easy access and he continues

to bite and lick my neck, driving me into a frenzy. His fingers move over my belly and up to my breasts. He pinches my nipples hard, making them stand to attention and I hear myself crying out as he pinches them again, this time hard enough to hurt.

I flinch and suck in a breath as he releases my nipples and the blood rushes to them, making them ache and sting. Finn ignores my discomfort, moving his hand down my body until his fingers push their way roughly into my panties and find my clit. He works my clit the same way he's worked the rest of my body; roughly. It's as though he's angry with himself for wanting this and he's taking his anger out on my body. My body responds, and I realize I am fucking loving this.

My cries of pain turn to moans of pleasure as Finn moves his fingers over my clit, bringing me almost to orgasm. Just when I am about to come, he moves his fingers away, leaving me frustrated. I growl in anger, but before I can react any further, Finn is pushing my head down, bending me over his desk.

He rips my panties away, tossing them to one side as they come apart in his hands. I hear a rustling sound, the sound of Finn finishing what I started and shoving his pants and boxers down.

I feel fire flood me as Finn's tongue finds my clit and runs through my lips to my pussy. He licks around the edge of my pussy, drinking in my juices, and then his tongue is gone, leaving me wanting more. I screech as he bites my ass cheek hard.

The pain mixes with the frustration and the pleasure and I feel myself coming undone, liquid drips from me as Finn's cock presses against my opening. He roughly shoves at my inner thighs and I don't need him to speak to understand what he's telling me. I step to the side with one leg, opening myself up to Finn, inviting him in.

He plunges into me and I cry out as he fills me, stretching me. He pounds into me, hard fast strokes that take my breath away. He presses down on my spine with one hand, forcing me to lay flat against his desk. The cold hard wood presses against my cheek as he pounds into me. He still holds me flat with one hand. His other hand is on my hip, pulling me back to meet his desperate thrusts. I need no encouragement. I throw myself against him, pushing against him, taking his full length inside of me, gasping and moaning as I stretch to accommodate his huge cock.

He ups the pace, banging into me, making every nerve ending in my body fire up at once. This time, he doesn't stop when I am on the edge and I go careening over and into the most intense orgasm, I've ever had. As I float through layers of pleasure that leave me gasping, Finn's hand leaves my hip. He moves it around to the front of my body and he pinches my clit so hard my moan becomes a scream as delicious agony fires through me.

My head comes up from the desk, my body still pressed flat and I scream Finn's name as pleasure fires through the center of me and spreads out in every direction at once. I gasp a breath and then I can't breathe anymore. My lungs burn, my body goes rigid. Every nerve is alive, overwhelming me with pleasure and for a moment, everything goes black and I feel my body sag.

The sensation passes, my vision rushing back in, making me dizzy, and my legs take my weight again. I manage to suck in a large, shuddering breath, which comes out in a low primal sound, the sound of an animal as Finn pinches my clit again. My body is thrown headlong into another all-consuming orgasm as I scream Finn's name over and over again while he pounds into me.

His hands move, both of them now on my hips, moving me faster and faster on his cock. I couldn't straighten up now even if I wanted to. My body is jelly, shaky, fantastic, mind blowing jelly.

Finn slams into me one more time, holding me in place, his cock so deep in me I can feel him pressing against my cervix. He comes hard, his cock going wild inside of me. He makes a deep, guttural sound and then he calls out my name. I feel a rush of warmth as he spurts deep inside of me.

And then he's gone, his cock slipping out of me. I start to straighten up, but my knees buckle beneath me and I start to tumble. Finn catches me in his arms and we fall to the ground together. I land on his lap then I turn and rest my head on his shoulder, my face pressed into his neck.

I can hardly breathe, and I know Finn is in a similar state of undone. His chest moves rapidly beneath me as his arms encircle me, holding me to him.

The moment of closeness between us is broken when Finn's office phone rings, a shrill, jarring sound that cuts through the noise of us trying to get our breath back. I know instinctively the moment is over and Finn will want to take the call. I shuffle awkwardly to the side, moving onto the carpet so he can get to his feet.

Finn pushes himself up, not even looking at me as he drags his boxers and pants back up. He reaches for the phone.

I push myself silently to my feet, grabbing my shredded panties and the book, then slip from the office unnoticed.

10

FINN

As my hand touches the receiver, the phone stops ringing. I know by how quickly the ringing stopped that it was nothing important. If it were, then the ringing would have kept going until I answered the call. I suspect it's a client or more likely an associate in a different time zone who realized how late it is here and hung up, planning on calling back at a less ungodly hour.

I take a moment to fasten my pants while I try to compose myself. I'm not quite sure what just happened. If someone had told me Ashley accidentally flashing her panties at me would be so distracting, I would have laughed at them. And if they'd told me her teasing me would lead to what just happened, I would have been hysterical with laughter. And yet here I was, in a world where both of those things just happened.

I turn around ready to say something, what I don't know, but something to Ashley. I'm torn between saying it can never happen again and asking her if she's ready to go again right

now. I'm saved from having to decide between the two senti-
ments when I see Ashley has gone. She must have made a
run for it when I went to take the call. It at least tells me
where she's at with this. She obviously thinks it was a
mistake. I mean, she's right.

It *was* a mistake.

But holy shit was it a mistake I enjoyed making!

I can't help but smile to myself when I think of what it felt
like to be inside of Ashley Winters. She drove me wild in a
way I never would have anticipated. But the speed with
which she left makes it obvious she clearly regrets it and
most probably doesn't want it to happen again.

I'm a little disappointed, a lot disappointed in fact, but it's
what we agreed to and I can't put pressure on Ashley to keep
on having sex with me if it's not what she wants. I'll have to
let it go.

I leave my office feeling strangely lost and go through to my
bedroom where I get out of my work clothes and go to the
bathroom. I shower and when I get out, I pull on a pair of
clean boxers. I stand brushing my teeth looking into the
mirror above the sink. I almost don't recognize myself.

It's not like I'm a typical Casanova type.

Okay, I used to be when I was younger and in college. That's
mostly what college is for, if anyone is being honest. Then I
grew up and started working for my grandpa, and somewhere along the way, work took over from dating. In fact,
work took over from pretty much everything. It became my
soul focus, over shadowing every other aspect of my life.

Maybe that's why this thing with Ashley feels so out of this world, so much more than just a quick fuck, because it's the first time in years I've done something so unexpected and unplanned, just because I wanted to. I didn't even use a fucking condom with her. I never do that!

Hell, I even missed a call because of it and didn't care. I would be lying if I said I normally would have missed a call. Even in the middle of the night, I'd have taken it, and if I hadn't been quick enough to get it, I would have called straight back instead of thinking the person would call me back during office hours if it were important.

It hit me now, with Ashley for the first time in as long as I could remember, I'd been fully immersed in the moment. I actually lost control and let my body take over. I don't think I've ever done that with a woman before. Scratch that, I know I haven't.

It's so strange that a woman I found almost unattractive in the beginning is the same woman who has knocked down my walls and made me feel like this. Like I'm spinning and out of control, but in the most delicious way imaginable.

Of course, it's typical that the first time I feel something like this, I know it can't happen again. Ashley has made it obvious she doesn't want it and besides, this is purely a business arrangement. I can't afford to go mixing up business and pleasure and getting them all confused in my head.

It isn't like I want a relationship with Ashley. Actually, I don't want a relationship with anyone right now, but especially not with someone like Ashley who makes me feel guilty for existing. And that's another good reason to not do it again.

The last thing I need is Ashley getting attached to me and starting to want more than I can give her.

None of the rationalizing I'm doing in my head convinces me that I don't want to fuck her again. I'd like nothing more than to go to her right now and take her all over again. I want to feel her lips around my cock, I want to plunge into her tight, wet little pussy and make her scream my name.

But I won't.

I can't.

Instead, I decide I do have to go to Ashley, but for a very different reason. We slipped up tonight, and we need to talk about that. I need to remind her of our rules then reiterate them and make it clear that anymore sex between us is well and truly off the table. It may be nothing for her, but I need a clear head.

I still feel a little bit strange when I think of Ashley. It's like now I've seen her in a whole new light. But I'm going to do this. I'm going to go and talk to her, because I'm not going to risk losing everything because our relationship gets complicated.

I march out of the bathroom like a man on a mission. I go straight through my bedroom, down the hallway to the guest room and knock on the door. I wait impatiently for her to answer. I'm debating knocking again when she calls out for me to come in. What took her so long? Is she trying to get up the courage to face me? Or maybe she's trying to compose herself because she thinks I want to fuck her again. Or maybe she's playing hard to get?

Jesus, what kind of mess am I getting myself into?

I shake my head and open the door.

Ashley is lying propped up in bed, the book from my office beside her on the pillow. She's using a tissue as a bookmark.

Although I try to deny it to myself, I have to admit it hurts a little to see her casually treat what happened between us as if it never bothered her in any way.

There she is reading a book like nothing happened between us and here I am boiling up with tension.

"What is it, Finn?" She asks with a sigh.

I realize I've been standing there staring at her like some fool. I clear my throat and move into the room.

11

ASHLEY

*F*inn and I had sex! Finn and I had sex!

I can't believe *I* made it happen. And without a condom? How stupid am I? I need my head examined. Worse still, is how damned much I enjoyed it. Heck, it was the best sex I've ever had.

There I said it. But I have to let it go, because it sure as hell can't happen again. This is a business arrangement, as simple as that, nothing more and nothing less, and I don't want any lines getting blurred.

Watching Finn stepping into my room wearing only a pair of boxers makes my whole body clench with desire. I take a moment to run my eyes over his chest, over the six pack I want to wash with my tongue, and then lower, my eyes automatically going to his cock.

I tell myself to stop it right now and move my eyes back up to Finn's face. He's just standing in the doorway staring at me, and I know that if I keep looking back at him, some-thing will happen again. It's written all over his face.

And I can't have that. He'll just have his fun and I'll be left nursing a broken heart.

"What is it Finn?" I ask with a sigh, as though he's disturbing me, as though I didn't just throw a tissue into the book beside me, so it looked like I'd been reading it. instead of being all torn up and restlessly pacing the floor.

Finn clears his throat when he realizes he is staring at me. He breaks eye contact and moves further into the room. He goes and takes a seat on the armchair in the corner, moving my clothes onto the dressing table top.

I can't decide if I'm relieved he's staying firmly out of my reach, or if I'm disappointed that he didn't come over, peel back the duvet, and fuck me all over again. Because that is what every fiber in my body craves.

"About what happened, Ashley. I shouldn't have let myself do that and I'm sorry."

I'm not, I think to myself. "Me too." I nod.

"Good. So then, we can both agree it was a mistake and it shouldn't happen again. I think we need to set some rules." Finn frowns. "I know we touched on this before, but that was at a time when neither of us thought we had to say no to having sex with each other. I think we both thought that to be a given at the time."

"Look Finn, no rules are necessary. We're adults. We fucked. It's done. We won't do it again. It's that simple."

"Right. Yeah. I guess you're right. We just won't do it again. We don't need to talk about it and make it a big deal." Finn is basically repeating back to me what I've just said to him.

Is it wrong that I'm kind of enjoying his discomfort? I know it's a little mean, but Finn never really struck me as the kind of guy who got flustered, especially not about something like this, and yeah, it's kind of amusing to watch. So sue me.

"And you're sure you're okay with this?" Finn asks. "Like it's not going to be weird between us, or anything now?"

"I'm sure. Mind you, if you don't let me get some sleep soon, I'm not sure how nice I'll be in the morning," I say, with a smile.

"Umm... we didn't use any protection..."

"Don't worry about it. I'm on birth control."

"Oh, okay. Well..." he doesn't look so flustered anymore.

But seeing him almost naked is starting to have an effect on me instead. An effect I most certainly don't want him to be aware of.

Finn gets to his feet. "Goodnight, Ashley."

"Night, Finn," I reply, but he has already closed the door, cutting off my words.

Yeah, it's going to be weird.

12

FINN

I still can't believe she was so fucking casual about it, like what we just did meant nothing at all to her. I also can't believe I'm not relieved about that. I should be relieved about it. She even made a joke about it, a joke clearly designed to get me out of her room.

I sigh into the darkness. I've been in bed for over an hour now and I'm no closer to getting to sleep than I was when I first came to bed. All I can see when I close my eyes is Ashley. All I can think about is how good it felt to be inside of her, how much she writhed beneath me, how hard we both came.

I can feel myself getting hard just thinking about it, so I try to think about something else. Instead of thinking about anything else, I see Ashley in my arms again. I blink away the image and then I see her propped up on her pillows telling me this can never happen again. It's not exactly a total change of thought patterns, but my cock as sure as hell backs off when I think of her rejecting me.

I punch the pillow and slam my head into it. I feel frustrated with myself.

I *wanted* her to agree that we couldn't do it again. I know it can't happen again, and I don't want to hurt Ashley, so I need her to be in agreement, but she agreed too damn easily for my liking. She dismissed me as if I was a used bar of soap.

And the fact she was quite contentedly reading a book bothers me more than it should. Like how can she just casually lay there reading, and not have these crazy thoughts plaguing her mind? I bet she's even asleep right now. And here I am, unable to get any sleep at all, because I can't damn well get her out of my mind.

I don't know what it's going to be like between us now. I know she said it won't be weird between us, and I want to believe her, but I don't think it's going to be her who makes it weird. I have a horrible feeling it'll be me.

I'm going to do my best to avoid Ashley as much as possible for the next few days. At least until I get her out of my mind and feel like I can be normal around her again.

IT'S BEEN two days since Ashley and I fucked.

It's pretty much all I've thought about in between meetings and calls. Yesterday morning, I heard her moving around from my office and I waited for the awkward moment when we bumped into each other for the first time, but minutes later, I heard the front door shut and she was gone.

She crept back in late, like after midnight late. And then this morning, she sneaked out at the crack of dawn again. If it had been weekdays, I would say it's been a coincidence that Ashley's just been working long hours. But it's the weekend so I know it is unlikely she has to stay out that much. The only explanation is she's decided to avoid me too.

In some ways, I'm relieved, but I've decided this ends tonight. This is ridiculous. We can't avoid each other forever, and the longer we leave it before we see each other again, the more awkward it's going to be between us.

I know my original plan was to avoid her, but I have no intention of seeing it through. By the time I woke up this morning I'd already decided to talk it out. See, I'm not a total asshole. I don't want her to feel uncomfortable being in my home, not when I've told her she's welcome to stay. I think if I plan it in such a way, so we bump into each other and get the awkwardness out of the way, then we'll be fine again.

We can go back to being... what? Friends? We were never really friends. Acquaintances? I'd like to think we were a little more than that. Business associates? Yes, that's probably the closest description of what we were. Whatever it was, we were just starting to be able to tolerate each other without snapping at each other's throats, and I'd like that back.

I'll force us to run into each other today. I finished up the few bits of work I had to do nice and early, because I don't want it to be obvious it's a forced plan. If I dart out of my office when I hear her come in, it'll be obvious I planned it that way. Instead, I'm sitting in the living room with the TV on as though it's just a normal evening and I'm watching a movie. Which if she knew me, she would know is something I never do. In fact, paying attention to the TV is really hard work and I have to force myself to sit here and endure the inane nonsense flirting across the scene.

It's after eleven when I hear Ashley's key rattling in the lock. I feel nervous suddenly, my palms sweating. I swallow hard and jump to my feet. I practically sprint to the mini bar and just manage to get behind it when the front door opens.

"Hey," Ashley calls, looking a little surprised to see me.

"Hi," I say. "Do you want a drink? You look like you've had a long day."

She does look like she's had a long day. Her face is pale, strained looking, and I can see how tired she is. She starts to shake her head, but then changes her mind. "I'd love one," she says softly. "A very large Cognac if you have one, please."

I nod and start to pour her a generous double as she puts her purse on the coffee table along with some files she is holding. Then she slips her coat off, lays it on the couch and takes her usual spot.

I decide I'm going to have a Cognac too. I carry our drinks over and mute the TV after I've handed her the drink.

She takes a good swallow of it. "Thanks," she smiles. "That really hit the spot." She nods at the TV. "You don't have to mute it on my account."

"I've seen it before, anyway." I shrug.

She nods and takes another sip of her drink. I wait for her to say something, but she doesn't. She just stares into space, sipping her drink. I don't know why she has this effect on me. If another woman decided not to talk, I'd just get up and get on with my day. With her, I can't do that. I didn't want to make a big deal out of this, but I want her to know it doesn't have to be this way. So I take a deep breath and plough into a semi-rehearsed speech I have been planning in case of this exact scenario, "Ashley, I told you that you were welcome to stay here and that you should make yourself comfortable," I start.

"And what? You changed your mind?" She interrupts me.

This annoys me. She has to be the most annoying person I know. "No. No, of course not. I was just going to say that you don't have to avoid me because of what happened. I want you to feel at home here."

"I appreciate that, Finn, and I do feel at home here. But I'm confused. Do you think I've been avoiding you or something?"

"Well, haven't you?" I challenge her. "You've been slipping out early, coming home late. And it's the weekend."

"You know, sometimes your arrogance surprises even me," she notes, shaking her head. "Believe it or not Finn, not everything is about you."

She says it with such venom in her voice that I'm actually shocked.

She shakes her head again, but this time, it must be at herself, because when she speaks again, her tone is softer,

"I'm sorry. I didn't mean that. I'm just a bit stressed out and I shouldn't have taken it out on you."

"It's fine," I reassure. I look at the almost empty glass in her hand. "Why don't I fix you another drink and then you can tell me what's bothering you."

"You wouldn't be interested," she says quietly.

I stand up and take the glass from her hand.

She looks up at me.

"Well, probably not, if it's not about me. But I can pretend to care," I quip.

Ashley gives a soft laugh and nods. "Fine, I'll tell you."

I go and pour her another drink and come back to the couch. I look at her, nodding for her to begin talking.

She is silent.

For a moment, I think she's changed her mind again.

Then she gives a soft laugh. "I don't even know where to start. It's just been one of those weekends where everything piles on, you know?"

I nod. I do know.

"It started with a furious phone call from our landlord because the rent for the office was late. I was able to deal with that courtesy of your check, so thank you for that."

"How late was your rent?" I ask, with a frown.

"Late," she says. "But not late enough to use all of the money you gave me. Anyway, once he left, I had a visit from a kid I'd never seen before. He told me he was worried about Alex, a kid who has been coming to us for a while now. He was getting clean, but the new kid thought he was going to slip up again after an unsuccessful meeting with his parents. He was right. By the time we found Alex, he'd overdosed. He's in the hospital now and they think he'll pull through, but it's just so... so sad."

"I'm sorry Ashley. That must have been hard." I sigh.

"It was. And you know the worst part? As I sat by that kid's bedside, praying he didn't die, in my mind, I was doing sums and reallocating funds, trying to work out if we had the resources to send him to rehab again. Don't worry, I'm not trying to up the game on you or anything like that."

I wince. I can only imagine the effect this must have had on her. "Ashley listen, if you need the rest of the money sooner—"

She cuts me off with a wry smile. "Why Finn Jagger, it's starting to sound almost like you care."

"Shit it is, isn't it?" I ask with a laugh. "I take it back."

She laughs with me and a little of the strain leaves her face.

I'd like to think it's because we're talking, but I suspect it's more to do with the Cognac. "Seriously though, it's there if you need it," I say.

"Thanks." She smiles. "But I spent all of yesterday evening rejigging things and I think that part at least is sorted."

"Good," I reply. "So it must have gotten better after that?"

"You would think, wouldn't you? But today has been almost

as bad. We lost a big donor this morning and then I decided to try and patch things up with my father. We were making some headway, and then I mentioned losing the donor and he flipped out, saying I'd only come to him for money. I hadn't. He's always made it clear that he doesn't support me in this and I would never ask him for money for it. Aside from anything, I know my father. He's the kind of man who would donate money and then assume he could tell me how to spend it, and frankly, I don't need that shit. So anyway, we got into another big argument. And then to top it all off, I had to have dinner with your mother earlier this evening to go over some of the wedding details."

"How was that?" I groan.

"Not as bad as I thought." Ashley smiles. "It shows you how bad this weekend has been when having dinner with a woman who absolutely terrifies me was the nicest part of it."

I try not to look too closely at what she's wearing, but I can't help it. Suddenly, it's clear she has made an effort with her clothes and I didn't even notice at first. She's wearing a fitted white blouse and a black pencil skirt. She's even wearing black heels. It's a safe, sensible outfit, but at least, she wouldn't have looked out of place wherever my mom dragged her.

Ashley smirks at me. "Yes, I learned from experience and bought something to wear for the dinner,"

I realize I haven't been as subtle as I thought I was. "It suits you."

She doesn't respond but her lips tilt up a bit as she brings her glass to her lips again.

"Dare I ask where we are with the wedding planning?" I ask quickly. The temperature in the room just rose by a few degrees.

"You can ask, but you'd need to call Damon or your mom if you want a halfway sensible answer. All I know for sure is I've chosen a champagne sponge cake with French vanilla buttercream and strawberry compote filling for our wedding cake. It's going to be five tiers and it'll be white with ruffles and edible silver leaf decorations."

"Ruffles?" I ask.

"You sound like me." She laughs. "They look nicer than they sound." She reaches up with one hand and rubs her neck, wincing slightly. "Oh, and I settled on Melbourne Hall for the location. I hope that's okay. The cathedral felt wrong knowing this is a sham, and your parents' house seemed too daunting."

"It's fine," I tell her. "You know, this is starting to feel like a real wedding."

She freezes and raises an eyebrow.

I laugh at her expression. "Well, isn't this how it goes? The bride makes the choices and the groom just agrees with everything." I chuckle.

Ashley laughs with me and nods. "Yeah, I guess you're right. I've got a dress fitting next week too and your mom has invited herself along so that's not going to be terrifying at all."

"Don't worry I'll get you out of it. Your own mom should be with you to get a wedding dress. Right?"

"Mmmm." She's still rubbing at her neck.

Something happens inside me. I take a big swallow of Cognac.

"She should be, but I haven't actually told her about the wedding yet, so I guess I'll just go with your mom. At least that way, there won't be any surprises on the big day if she hates the dress."

I nod absently, not paying much attention to her words now. My eyes keep going to her hand on her neck. "Have you hurt your neck?" I ask, trying and failing not to be distracted by the way her hand kneads her skin and the way her collar is coming more and more open.

"I just have a knot there. It always happens when I'm stressed out."

"Turn around and I'll get it for you," I offer without thinking.

Ashley raises an enquiring eyebrow at me.

"Oh, come on Ashley. It's not like I'm suggesting we have sex. Surely, you trust yourself to let me massage your neck."

She looks at me for a second too long, then nods, and turns her back towards me.

I shuffle closer to her and raise my hands, suddenly afraid to touch her.

"Come on, Finn. It's not like you're jumping out of a plane or anything," she teases with a chuckle.

Her tone is light and teasing and there's that chuckle to end it all, but I can still hear the tension behind it and I know she feels it too. The way the air in the room is suddenly charged. And the certainty that if I put my hands on her, this isn't going to stop with a massage.

I reach out and gently push her collar further down, exposing her creamy white skin. I place my hands on her shoulders and work my thumbs against her neck. My skin tingles where it touches hers and when she moans under my touch, I feel my cock getting hard. I ignore the desire I can feel spreading through me, reminding myself how we both agreed this can't, won't and shouldn't happen again. I try to tell myself it's just a natural response, a primal thing really... it means nothing.

I don't believe it at all.

Ashley isn't helping matters at all. She's opened a few more buttons of her blouse and pushed her blouse further down her back and arms, exposing the milky white skin there. Then she pushes the straps of her bra down her arms.

My cock jerks in my pants. Shit. Suddenly, her exposed skin, my fingers rubbing firmly into her flesh, that small involuntary sound she makes, feel taboo and... like the hottest thing I have ever done.

Ashley moans again and a wave of desire pounds through me. I know then that I can't do this. I stand up abruptly. "Right, that should do the trick." I start to walk away, but her hand grabs my wrist, stopping me and turning me to face her. Her eyes go to my crotch and I know she can see how hard my dick is. I wait for the accusation I know is coming, how we said this wouldn't happen again, but Ashley surprises me once more. She doesn't accuse me of anything. She doesn't speak at all.

Instead, she pulls me towards her.

She releases my wrist and her hands go to my sweatpants. She pulls them down together with my boxers.

"Ashley..." I start as my cock is released from its material prison. The words die in my throat when she moves to the edge of the couch and stretches her lips around my cock. As she moves her mouth down my length, I couldn't protest even if I wanted to. I groan as her tongue moves over the tip of my cock, flicking back and forth and sending shockwaves through me.

Then she sucks my cock deep into her mouth, and putting her hands on my ass cheeks, pulls me roughly closer to her. She keeps a tight hold on my ass as her head begins to bob, faster and faster, her rhythm perfect.

I am moaning and gasping with each breath now as Ashley pushes me towards the edge. I can feel my stomach clenching, my cock going wild. I reach down and push my hands into her hair, moving her head even faster.

She doesn't resist my direction; she just ups her pace.

My mouth hangs open, my eyes are closed, and my head's thrown back as I feel my climax building in the base of my cock. Suddenly her hot, wet, velvety mouth is gone. Where there was warmth, there is now a chilly breeze.

I open my eyes and look down at Ashley.

She looks back up at me, a wicked grin on her face. She runs her tongue over her lips and makes an *ahh* sound that makes me growl in frustration. She gives a soft laugh and stands up.

For one awful second, I think this is over, but Ashley has other ideas. She hitches her skirt up over her hips and pushes her panties down, kicking them away.

She sits back down on the couch and grabs my t-shirt, pulling me down on top of her as she lays back. My lips meet hers and her tongue moves into my mouth as our kiss becomes passionate, desperate. I can taste myself on her tongue as our tongues entwine. I move my mouth from hers and kiss the side of her neck.

Her hands push beneath my t-shirt, moving over my back, sending shivers through me. She drags the t-shirt off me, throwing it over the back of the couch. "Fuck me, Finn," she orders in a low husky voice.

I don't need telling twice. In this moment, I barely remember why we thought this was a bad idea. How can anything feel this good, be anything but a good idea?

I reach down and run my fingers through her slit, moaning when they come away dripping wet. Ashley is as ready for this as I am, and I don't waste any more time. I push my cock into her wet, tight pussy and begin to move my hips. Ashley wraps her legs around my waist, opening herself up to me and letting me go in deeper.

As heat envelopes my body and pleasure floods my veins, I let go of any concerns and just enjoy the moment. I am already close to coming, Ashley made sure of that when she took me into her juicy mouth. Ashley is close too. I can tell by the way her breathing has grown ragged, by the way her hands are all over me, like she wants to caress every single spot on my back, my sides.

I lean down and kiss her, a hungry kiss that makes her moan into my mouth. I move my hips faster as I feel my orgasm starting to take over. There's no going back now and I moan loudly. As I start to come, I feel Ashley's pussy clench and she screams my name, coming with me. We both come hard, a blending of juices, and moans.

I feel my muscles tightening as I hit the peak of my climax and then I relax, my muscles turning to jelly, my heart beating hard.

Ashley shifts slightly on the couch so I can fit in beside her. We lay on our sides, facing each other, our eyes searching each other's faces.

I know I should move, go to bed or something, but right now, I feel too tired to move. I wrap an arm around Ashley and kiss her forehead. I wait for her to pull away as I kiss her head, to start telling me we made another mistake and run from the room, but she doesn't. She snuggles closer to me, wrapping her own arm around me.

This feels dangerous, like more of a mistake than the actual sex, but I don't care. It feels good to lay here beside Ashley and when my eyes start to close, I don't fight it, I just let myself fall asleep in her arms.

13

ASHLEY

As I wake up, I try to stretch, but I feel like I'm confined. I open my eyes and see Finn lying so close to me that almost every inch of our bodies are touching. Last night rushes back in.

We had sex again. Sex that I instigated. Right here on the couch. After the sex, we laid in each other's arms, something that felt awfully a lot like crossing the most forbidden of lines.

Sex with Finn and me, is rough, fast and hard, and while we're doing that, I can convince myself it's just physical. That we're just fucking. But laying in each other's arms after it? It feels tender, like something two people who want to do more than just fuck each other's brains out would do.

I could see how tired Finn looked after we fucked and I knew he wouldn't be awake for long. I remember smiling to myself, telling myself I had worn him out. I felt pretty tired myself, but I told myself I would just wait for Finn to fall asleep before I would disentangle myself from his arms and legs then go to bed.

Except when he did fall asleep, I found I didn't want to move. I told myself I was just waiting a while, to make sure he was in a deep enough sleep, so I wouldn't wake him up and have to have an awkward conversation with him, but I knew it wasn't really that.

The truth is, it felt nice lying there in his arms, and I didn't want to move away. Now, I wish I had. Because this is a mistake. A huge mistake. We've crossed a major line here. We really should have just stuck to avoiding each other. It seemed to be working out pretty well for us. That's what we're going to have to go back to doing.

I gently lift Finn's arm up and very carefully slip out from beneath it. I get to my feet, holding my breath for a moment, praying he won't wake up.

He rolls onto his front and makes a little snorting sound.

I can't stop looking at him. He looks soft and vulnerable— like a man I would want for myself. Forever.

Then his breathing settles down again, and he stays asleep.

Thank God, for small mercies.

I pull my skirt down, unrolling it from around my hips and pull my blouse up onto my shoulders then fasten one button to hold it in place. I look around for my panties and find them poking out from beneath the couch. I scoop them up and start to creep out of the room, but I can't resist stopping for a moment to watch Finn.

He's still on his front, his head turned to the side. He looks like all of his worries have floated away. He must have kicked his sweat pants and boxers right off in the middle of the night because he's completely naked now. I can't help but notice how good he looks. And then my mind wanders back to last night, to how he made my body feel alive like no one ever has before.

It's a dangerous thought and I find myself tempted to run my hands over his body, to wake him up and ride him hard. But of course, I don't. Instead, I turn around and practically run from the room before I do something else I'm going to regret.

I go through to my room and hop into the shower. I'm conscious of the tenderness between my legs, a physical reminder of how big and thick Finn is. I ignore the thoughts crowding my mind and focus on the day ahead of me. I have a couple of meetings today, meetings which could decide the fate of the charity, so I should be giving them my complete and undivided attention.

I get dressed, pulling on a black pantsuit with a pale blue blouse, then adding a pair of black flats. I know Finn wouldn't approve of this outfit. What was it he said? Oh yes, I dress like I'm actually trying to repel people. Clearly, it didn't work on him.

I grin at this thought, then I push Finn from my mind and go to stand in front of the mirror. Regardless of his opinion, I know this outfit is the right choice. It says professional, but it doesn't say I spend thousands of dollars on clothes, because what sort of message does it send when the person running a charity could support half of her charges simply by selling some of her designer clothes?

I check the time and I'm shocked to see it's barely five in the morning. I knew it was early, but this is really early. Finn is always in the office by seven. I debate sitting in the armchair in the corner of my room and reading my book for a bit. I smile to myself when I realize I had no trouble falling asleep without it last night.

I shake my head, trying to stop thoughts of Finn infiltrating my every other thought. I decide against sitting down with the book. I'm just going to go to the office early and prepare for my meetings. There'll be other stuff I can do as well, there always is and at the office I'm not risking running into a naked, disheveled and sexy as fuck Finn.

This last thought does it and I flee. I hurry through the living room, barely glancing at Finn. As noiselessly as I can I grab my purse and the files I brought home last night. I am at the door of the apartment by the time I allow myself to glance back at Finn just one more time.

I smile to myself as I stand and watch him for a moment. He hasn't moved since I left him and I still find myself wanting to go to him, to wake him with a kiss. I slip out of the apartment before I let myself do it.

It hits me as I run to the elevator so hard that I come to a dead stop. I don't regret sleeping with Finn because I don't like him. I regret it because I'm slowly starting to fall for him. I take a deep breath. This can lead to only one thing. Me getting hurt. I have to go back to avoiding him until I figure out some way to stop myself from falling more and more deeply in love with him. And I think, or at least I hope, it's not too late for that.

14

ASHLEY

I've done a good job of avoiding Finn over the last couple of days. It's day three since our episode on the couch, and I've managed to slip in and out for work, staying later at the office each night and going in earlier each day, without running into Finn. He works long hours himself and it's been surprisingly easy to time it, so we don't have to see each other. I've even caught up on a lot of those pesky admin tasks that need doing but aren't a priority and tend to get ignored, so it's been a win, win situation for me.

Tonight though, I'm so tired I decide to just come back home, and yes, I'm now starting to think of Finn's place as home. It's almost six and I know Finn isn't due to come home for at least another four or five hours so I feel pretty safe when I decide to go to the kitchen and grab a soda. Finn wasn't kidding about not keeping food in the apartment, but he has a surprisingly varied range of drinks and not just alcoholic ones.

I slip into my new pajamas, I bought a pair and returned

Finn's shirt, then head out to the kitchen. I'm humming to myself as I pull the fridge door open and look at the soda. I settle for a can of sparkling pineapple juice. I straighten up and close the fridge.

"Hey," Finn calls from behind me.

Shit. Fuck.

"Hey," I call, smiling as I turn around while hopefully hiding my surprise at him being here. "I didn't hear you come in."

"I was in ninja mode." Finn grins.

"Clearly." I laugh as I lift the soda can awkwardly. "I was just grabbing a drink. So I'll... I guess... just go back to my room."

He starts to say something, but he changes his mind and nods.

I scuttle out of there as fast as I can without actually running and I don't stop moving until I'm back in my room. I close the door and lean against it for a moment, sighing loudly.

I stupidly hoped that when Finn and I did see each other again, that I would feel differently about him. Not see him as being hot anymore. Go back to seeing him as the arrogant douchebag I thought he was when we first met. But the thing is, I can't see him like that anymore. Now don't get me wrong, he is still arrogant. In fact, he's one of the most arrogant men I've ever met, but there's more to him than that.

Beneath the arrogant exterior, there's a genuinely nice guy. When he forgets to be a dick, he really isn't one. Like the other night when he could see I was stressed out, so he gave me a drink and a shoulder rub. And I don't think for a second he was trying to seduce me. In fact, when he realized the effect the massage was having on him, he tried to leave and it was me who stopped him.

It was me... who seduced him.

Or like the afternoon we spent in the soup kitchen. I really saw a different side to him there. He tried to play it cool, to act like he was only doing it because he had something to prove, but I saw the way he was with the kids, the way their stories moved him. He'd acted compassionate and sweet then afterwards, when he caught himself showing his softer side, he started talking about buying a new shirt, I knew what he was doing. He acted like a dick again because for a moment, he'd been stripped bare and allowed me to see who he really was.

So yeah, my plan to see Finn and not feel anything anymore is well and truly dead so to speak. I move away from the door and go to perch on the end of my bed.

So here's the deal, I tell myself. *You like Finn. You let yourself go there. And you can let yourself not go there just as easily. You can't help liking him, but you can help acting on it. Acting on it is only going to get you hurt. Finn might not be who you thought he was, but he isn't really into you and if you give yourself on a platter to any man, he is going to take it. Then if you keep on letting him fuck you, he's going to break your heart.*

It really isn't fair to either of us if I let anything happen between us again. It isn't fair to me because I will get hurt. It isn't fair to Finn because inevitably, it will paint him as the bad guy when I get my heart broken. It won't be his fault, as far as he is concerned, I still hate him, but as much as I know he's not into me, I don't think he would like to think he was hurting me.

I am just going to do what I had already planned to do this evening. Relax with my book for a bit and then have an early night. I tell myself I can ignore the fact that Finn is in his office, just a few doors down from me.

I grab my book and move to the armchair, taking my soda with me. I open the can and take a long drink. It is sweeter than I expected it to be and I pull a face, but it is kind of refreshing in its own way, and when I take another drink, I realize I quite like it. I nod to myself, set it on the top of the chest of drawers beside me and open my book. I have read all of two lines when there is a knock on my door.

My heart stops beating. I sigh quietly and remind myself this isn't Finn's fault. He doesn't know why I am avoiding him. He probably just thinks I feel awkward about what happened the other night. I do a little bit, but that's being totally overshadowed by this stupid crush I seem to have developed. Am I really so pathetic that a guy only has to make me come and I'm putty in his hands?

Apparently so.

I get up and go to open the door. Shouting for him to come in feels too much like an invitation for more. I steel myself and pull the door open. Finn is no longer in his suit and tie. He is wearing a pair of fashionable looking jeans and a white t-shirt. He smiles when I open the door and I feel my pussy clench.

"Get changed," Finn says. "I'm taking you out for dinner."

His comment should piss me off. It wasn't so much an invitation as it was a demand. Yet, I suddenly find it hard to be mad with him. I still wasn't about to go on a date with him though, because as much as that is what I would want it to be, I know to him it won't be that. I shake my head. "I'll take a rain check. I'm kind of tired and I was just going to have an early night."

"Ok, another time then," he replies.

He starts to move away from the door, but he looks so crestfallen it makes me feel awful. He is trying to alleviate any awkwardness between us, and I'm making it worse. I know what's happening here. I'm letting my sudden crush on him make me act out and I don't much like myself when I become that person. "Finn, wait," I call.

He turns back, looking hopeful.

"I'm really not up for getting dressed up and going out, but if you order in, we could hang out."

He smiles at me, a warm, totally masculine, drop dead gorgeous smile. "Sounds good to me. I need to make a quick phone call. Why don't you go grab the menus and see what sounds good?"

I smile and nod. Maybe this will be okay after all. There isn't any awkwardness between us, and I am a grown woman dammit. I can control myself.

I watch Finn heading for his bedroom and then I make my way through to the living room. I keep going, heading to the kitchen, opening the top drawer, and pulling out a handful of menus. I go and sit down at the dining room table. I flick through the menus then begin sorting them into a maybe and a definite no pile. I narrow my maybe pile down into two menus and jump slightly when I notice Finn standing beside me.

"Will you stop sneaking around?" I laugh nervously.

He pulls out a chair and sits down at the table. "But it's so much fun startling you," he mocks

I roll my eyes good naturedly and point to the two menus. "I'm torn between Mexican and Thai. What do you like?"

"I could go for some Thai."

"Then it's settled then. Thai, it is," I say.

Finn picks up the Thai menu. "Should I order their dragon surprise meal and we'll have a bit of everything?"

Seeing his long eyelashes rest on his cheek makes my heart flutter and I nod speechlessly when he looks up at me.

Finn moves away from the table and goes out onto the balcony where he paces up and down as he talks on the phone. He's changed into a pair of navy blue tracksuit bottoms and a different t-shirt. The t-shirt is big on him the kind you wear when you just want to be comfortable.

It makes me feel slightly better about the fact I'm still wearing my pajamas.

Finn comes back inside a few minutes later, sliding the door closed behind him.

"You know, even when you're just ordering food you pace about like you're in the middle of a major call," I point out.

He grins. "It is a major call. I'm hungry."

I laugh and shake my head.

He heads over to the mini bar. "Do you want a drink?"

"I'd love a glass of rose if you have any."

"Your wish is my command," he drawls with a wink.

If only.

He bends down to the little fridge beneath the bar and comes out with a dark bottle. He opens it with a flourish, even though it's a screw cap, and pours me a large glass full. He pours himself a whiskey and nods towards the living room area.

I get up and follow him to the couch, instantly aware of what happened last time we were sitting here.

Finn hands me my glass and smiles at me. "We return to the scene of the crime."

I feel myself blushing slightly and I take a drink of the wine rather than having to respond to him. I mean what would I even say?

"Look Ashley, when we first met, we didn't much like each other and we were both sure that wouldn't change. But I think it has. I think we've both seen sides to each other that we didn't know were there and it's changed things slightly. And clearly, we do find each other attractive." He pauses and smiles at me.

I return his smile, wondering where the hell he's going with this. It occurs to me that even if he feels the same way as I do and is going to talk about us maybe making a go of this... I don't want that. It will be too complicated with everything else going on between us.

"We said we don't need rules, but it looks like maybe we do. Obviously, it wasn't enough to say we won't have sex again," he adds.

"Wait," I interrupt him. "Did you ask me to have dinner with you just to dump me?"

"I... um... no," he falters staring at me in disbelief.

His expression is priceless and I can't keep the laugh in any longer. It bursts out of me in a rush.

Finn looks confused for a moment and then he laughs too. "You totally got me there," he admits. "But seriously, I do think we need some ground rules."

I nod for him to go on. He's probably right and I'm interested to know where he's going with this.

"I also think saying we'll never ever have sex just makes us want it more. So here's what I propose," he goes on. "We make a no sex rule just for one night. For tonight only, we can't have sex with each other. We can talk and get to know each other a little better, but sex is off the table. And we can revisit the rule in the morning."

"I like it." I nod. "Saying never is a lot of pressure. But we're not animals. We can make it through one night without anything happening between us."

"Exactly," Finn agrees.

"Ok, deal." I raise my glass.

Finn clinks his glass against mine.

"To one night of platonic bonding." I grin like a Cheshire cat.

"Oh, I love it when you talk dirty," Finn teases with a laugh.

We each swallow a mouthful and seal the deal.

I feel better now, more relaxed. I don't know if it's because there's suddenly no pressure for tonight, or if it's because Finn didn't take sex entirely off the table, but whatever it is, I like this relaxed feeling.

There is no tension between us and we begin to chat about our days, about Finn's business and my charity. We move onto talking about the most random things. When the food arrives, we're deep into a debate about whether or not Die Hard is a Christmas movie or not. It clearly isn't, but Finn is convinced it is.

We spread the food out across the table and eat it straight out of the boxes, still chattering away the whole time. By the time we finish eating, and Finn puts some music on, I realize I am more than halfway down my bottle of rose wine. I know I should ease up on it a little bit, but I'm having a good time and I decide to cut myself a break. It's not like I'm falling over drunk. I'm just happy and relaxed.

I jump to my feet, run to Finn's side and grab his hands. "Dance with me."

"Dance with you?"

I nod, pulling him into the open space between the living room and the dining table. "Yeah. You know that thing people do to music where they move around and have fun? Come on, show me some of your moves. I want to see what you'll be like at our wedding." I laugh at his expression. I think he is going to say no, but he spins me away from him so swiftly, pulls me back to him, and dips me down so fast I get dizzy.

"That's pretty much my only move," he jokes with a grin.

"It's a good one though," I say, grabbing him tightly. I am still dipped and I'm acutely conscious of Finn's arm around my back, my hand in his. It's as though my realization is infectious because Finn pulls me back up and steps away from me. I curse myself inside for taking a good night like this and making it awkward.

Finn turns back to me and rather than looking like he feels uncomfortable, he's grinning. "Right I humored you and did your dance thing. Now it's your turn to humor me."

Just like that, the awkward moment passes.

I laugh and shake my head. "Ok, I'll humor you," I slur, wondering where the hell he's going with this. "What exactly are you suggesting?"

"Isn't it obvious?" he asks rolling his eyes. He moves away from me and begins to shove one of the couches around in a half circle, moving it towards the back of the other one. He looks back over his shoulder at me and grins again. "Blanket fort."

"You want us to make a blanket fort?" I ask, sure I must have misunderstood.

Finn pushes the couch into position so it sits back to back with the other one, a gap of a couple of feet between them. He begins to pull the cushions off the couch and lay them down in the gap. "For God's sake, don't stand there pretending like you don't want to do this," Finn taunts.

And he's right. I do want to do this. I haven't done anything like this since I was a little kid, and it just feels right. I laugh and run towards the hallway.

"I knew it!" Finn shouts after me.

I'm still laughing when I return from the linen closet with a large sheet and four big fluffy pillows. We drape the sheet over the backs of the couches, forming a tunnel between them. I clamber into the gap and begin to arrange the pillows. I hear Finn moving away and I peer out. He disappears down the hallway, so I crawl back out of the tunnel and start to add more couch cushions.

Finn comes back with a small lamp. He pulls an extension cord out from beneath the TV and stretches it over to the fort. He puts it behind the pillows and switches it on. "Get your wine and go in there." He grins then disappears again.

I do as he says. I'm nestled amongst the cushions with my glass when he returns.

He turns the light off, leaving only the lamp on and he crawls into the space beside me with a fluffy blanket in his hands which he spreads over us.

"You forgot your drink," I remind.

"No drinks in the fort," he cautions. "I made an exception for you."

"No exceptions necessary." Knowing I'm already seriously tipsy, I still drain my glass before shuffling to the end of the blankets to reach up and put the glass on the coffee table. I crawl back in and lay back on the cushions.

Finn lays beside me, his hands folded beneath his head. "When was the last time you just forgot about all of your responsibilities and did something like this just for the sheer fun of it?" He asks.

I think for a moment and I shake my head. "I honestly can't remember."

"Me neither," Finn agrees. "That's pretty fucking sad, isn't it?"

"Yeah, I guess it is. I just... I don't know. Somehow it always feels wrong to let go and enjoy myself when I think of all of the work I have piling up."

"Same here," Finn replies. "At least, you're helping people though. I mean I'm depriving myself of a bit of downtime for what? To make money?"

"Don't be fooled, Finn. I like helping people, but really, this whole thing started because I needed to do something to fill the void inside of myself," I admit. "It might be helping people, but it's kind of selfish too."

Finn shuffles onto his side and rests his head on his palm, propped up on his elbow. He looks down at me. "I don't think you're selfish at all. Even if you get something out of what you do, you're doing so much for so many people, and it can't be easy."

I find myself looking back up at him. "You know, for a moment there, that actually sounded like you gave me a compliment," I tease him.

"Yeah, it's just the whiskey talking. Don't worry, it won't happen again." He flops back down onto his back folding his hands beneath his head again.

"Noted." I grin. "So before any of this, did you ever see yourself getting married?"

"I didn't really think about it to be honest. Obviously, I wanted to find the right girl and settle down... one day. But it certainly wasn't something I was planning on doing any time soon. What about you?"

"I never really saw the point of getting married. I mean if you love someone enough to want to spend forever with them, do you really need a contract to prove it?" I ask.

"You see marriage as a contract? Even outside of this situation?" Finn asks, surprised.

I nod. "Well, yeah. Don't you? I mean think about it. You make these promises and you sign a contract to say you're legally bound to another person and you need another piece of legal document to say you are no longer bound."

"Your lawyer stripes are showing through. You guys sure know how to suck the romance out of anything. I like to think of it as more of a public celebration of your love for each other."

"Sap," I mocks with a laugh.

"Cynic," he shoots back.

"You know, maybe this was your grandfather's plan all along," I suggest. "To bring us together and force us to change our views on marriage. You know, I can make you a bit more practical about it, and you can make me a bit more romantic about it."

"Or maybe he just knew we would never find anyone to put up with our bullshit, unless he made it happen."

"Actually, yeah, that sounds much more like it," I agree.

We fall into a comfortable silence and I try to work out what Finn's grandpa really wanted this marriage to achieve. Did he think we would be a good match simply because he and my grandfather were friends? Which sounds silly. Or maybe he somehow sensed we would never get past our prejudices and see it for ourselves unless we were pushed together? Or did he really think that we were so bad a match that making Finn try to convince me to marry him would be a true test of how far he is willing to go to save the company?

I give up trying to puzzle it out. I don't think even Finn fully understands his grandpa's reasoning behind this, and he knew the man a hell of a lot better than I did. I turn my head to speak to Finn. His eyes are closed. I don't think he's asleep, but I don't think he's far from it either. It is getting pretty late. "We should go to bed," I say.

He turns towards me, opens one eye, and smiles at me. "We can't. Remember our rule?"

"I meant separately," I clarify with a soft laugh.

"We can't anyway," Finn shrugs.

"Oh? And why is that?" I ask.

"Because it's the first rule of a blanket fort. Once you build it, you have to sleep in it," Finn says like this is obvious.

"And that's an official rule, is it?" I ask with a raised eyebrow.

"Sure. At least it is now. My fort, my rules." He closes his eye again and spreads his arm out.

I debate what to do and in the end, I think what the hell. I snuggle closer to Finn, turning onto my side and resting my head on his chest. He wraps his arm around me and I put my palm on his stomach, feeling it moving up and down with his breathing.

"I knew you'd see sense," he mumbles, his voice thick with sleep.

"Well, I'd hate to break the rules of the fort. You know, since you put so much thought into them."

He grunts in response and then he falls silent.

His breathing becomes deeper and I know he is asleep now. I debate sneaking away, but I decide against it. I lay awake for a long time, listening to Finn's deep, even breaths, just enjoying being so close to him, knowing it's a dangerous move and not caring.

I decide for one night to just enjoy this new-found closeness between us and stop worrying about what tomorrow might bring. I'll worry about tomorrow when tomorrow comes.

I must have fallen asleep eventually, because I wake up still in the fort. The lamp is no longer on and I know instantly I'm alone in the fort and I feel a little sad, like the magic from last night has gone. Finn obviously woke up and slipped away so he didn't have to face me in the morning. I can't even be mad at him for it after I did the same thing to him the other morning.

I sit up and stretch and then I crawl out of the fort. I stand still and listen, but the apartment is silent. Finn has gone to work. I shrug, telling myself it shouldn't matter, but somehow it does. I shake the thought away and head for the kitchen where I can smell coffee. I touch the pot. It's still warm. I open up the cupboard above the machine and grab my favorite mug. I pull it down and spot a sheet of paper rolled up inside of it. I pull it out with a frown. My frown turns to a smile when I unfold it and see it's a note from Finn. I'm still smiling when I read it.

Sorry I had to run out. Even the magic of the fort can't stop office emergencies. See you tonight, Finn x.

Okay, so maybe he didn't run away so he didn't have to face me, and maybe we haven't quite lost the magic from last night.

I pour myself a coffee and sit down at the counter to drink it. I know nothing can happen between us and I'm slowly making my peace with that, but I like how Finn and I can connect on some level as friends.

15

FINN

I felt bad this morning about having to run out on Ashley, but I had an early morning video conference scheduled, like really early, and I didn't want to wake her. I knew she would find my note and know I hadn't run out on her, just that something came up I had to deal with. I almost left the note beside the coffee machine, but on a whim, I tucked it into her favorite mug instead.

Because of my super early start, I don't feel guilty leaving the office at six instead of a stupidly late time. I figure Ashley will get in around half an hour after me now, since we're no longer trying to avoid each other. Maybe we can have dinner together again. Or maybe tonight, she will feel like going out to eat.

I don't bother changing. I'll wait and see what she wants to do first before I decide what to wear. I sit down on the couch and then it hits me. I like Ashley. Not just desire her, not just like the way I feel when I'm fucking her. I actually like her as a person. I want to spend time with her even if nothing happens between us.

I watch the clock impatiently as it moves towards seven. Then eight. Then nine. I've tried to call Ashley a few times, but it keeps going to voicemail. I'm starting to get really worried now and I debate calling Tyson and have him track Ashley down. That would be weird though if it's just something's come up at work and she stayed late at the office to deal with it. But what if it isn't that? What if something has happened to her?

It's 9:25 when she finally comes in. I stand up and open my mouth to ask if she's okay when I realize she's not alone. She's with a man. A tall man who isn't bad looking and who seems to be hanging on her every word as they laugh together.

I instantly hate him.

"Oh Finn, hi. We're not disturbing you, are we?" Ashley asks.

It takes every bit of will power I have not to tell her to go to hell and take her douchebag date with her, but I manage to arrange my face into what I hope is a careless smile and shake my head instead.

"This is Alan Gershwin," Ashley introduces. "Alan, Finn Jagger."

Alan steps forward and offers me his hand.

I shake it, because what else am I supposed to do? Wrench his arm behind his back and boot him out of my apartment? That's what I'm itching to do.

"How's it going?" He asks, with a sick grin.

"Busy," I mutter

"I'll go and grab the file. I won't be a moment," Ashley says before she disappears down the hallway, leaving me and Alan alone together.

We stand in uncomfortable silence, watching each other cautiously. Yeah, I hate him. And I really fucking hate the fact that I am jealous of him. I try not to glare at him. We stand staring each other down.

"So Finn, what do you do?" He asks awkwardly.

I have half a mind to ask him to mind his own business.

Fortunately, Ashley breezes back in, stopping any conversation in its tracks. "Here you go," she smiles, handing Alan a file.

He takes the file and thanks her.

"Would you like to stay for a drink?" She asks.

I jump in before Alan can answer, "Umm... aren't you forgetting something?"

"What?" Ashley asks with a frown. She seems to be completely oblivious to the atmosphere between Alan and I.

"We have the wedding stuff to go over," I slip in smoothly.

"Wedding stuff?" Alan interrupts. His face turns quite pale. "Ashley, you didn't tell me you were getting married."

No, I bet she fucking didn't.

Ashley opens her mouth to say something, shooting me a

look that feels like it should have turned me to stone or something. She forces a smile. "Yes, I am Alan."

"Uh... right. Well, I'll pass on the drink, thanks. I'd hate to stand in the way of your perfect wedding."

Ashley sees the mumbling fool out. As soon as she closes the door, she rounds on me. "What exactly the fuck was that?" She demands.

"What was what?" I ask, feigning innocence. "My mom called earlier. She needs to know whether we want the salmon or chicken entrée."

"And you don't think that could have been a conversation we could have had five minutes after Alan left?"

"You didn't tell him we were getting married?" I ask pointedly, ignoring what she said.

"No, I didn't, because I haven't even told my parents yet, Finn. Jeez, I can't believe you did that. Now he's going to think I deliberately kept it a secret from him," Ashley yells.

"Well, you did," I point out. "Why do you care so much what he thinks anyway?"

"Dammit Finn, I can't even talk to you right now. You choose the damned entrée and tell your mother your choice. As if I care." She starts to storm away from me.

I grab her arm and spin her back around to face me. "Where the hell have you been?" I demand. "I was worried about you."

"Worried about me? It's not even ten o'clock," she points out.

Ok, she has a point there. I have completely overreacted about her being late. "I tried to call you and you ignored my calls," I say.

"My phone was on silent mode in my purse. I didn't hear it ringing."

That makes me even madder. "So where were you?"

"That's none of your goddamned business," she snaps, anger flaring over her face again.

"The last time you disappeared like this, you were in trouble," I point out.

"And this time, I wasn't. I'm a fucking grown woman Finn, and if I want to stay out past nine o'clock, I don't expect it to be a problem."

"Yeah? Well, I don't expect you to bring strange men back to the apartment," I snap.

"Oh, that's what this is about," Ashley says. "It's not about where I've been, but who I was there with."

I shrug, not quite ready to admit to this, but seeing no feasible way to deny it.

"Not that it's any of your business, but Alan is an old friend from college. He thinks he can help with one of my cases, hence the file. We haven't seen each other in a long time so we went out to grab a bite to eat together. And you have nothing to worry about, Finn. I wasn't on a date, making you look like a laughing stock. Alan is very happily married."

"I... oh," I say, the wind going out of my sails. "Fuck. I'm sorry Ashley. I just... I don't even know what it is."

"You're sorry?" she asks sarcastically. "Well, that's okay then. I mean it's not like you've made one of my oldest friends think I was hiding my fiancé away like a dirty secret. And it's not like you were so rude to him that he practically ran away from me, is it?"

"I'm sorry," I mutter, angrier with myself than she is.

"Yeah? Well that's not good enough. Why did you even behave that way Finn?" Ashley shouts.

"Because I was jealous alright?" I shout back. I don't give her time to respond. I close the gap between us, grab her, pull her into my arms, and kiss her hard on the mouth.

She goes stiff for a second and then she kisses me back, her arms wrapping around me. She pulls back slightly. "Aren't we meant to make a new rule for today?" She asks breathlessly.

"Fuck the rules," I reply, pulling her mouth back to mine. This isn't what I meant to happen tonight or any other night for that matter, but now that it is, I'm certainly not going to try and stop it. I don't think I could even if I wanted to. Angry sex with Ashley is easily the highlight of my year.

Hell, of my fucking life.

I start to walk her backwards as we kiss, slamming her against the wall behind her. She makes an animal sound, but it doesn't stop her from kissing me, from pushing my jacket off, unbuttoning my shirt and pushing that off too. She's opening my slacks and I'm tearing at her blouse, finally getting it open and discarding it.

The rest of our clothes come off in a frenzied movement, our mouths only leaving each other long enough to strip each other naked. It's like we're driven by lust, not stopping to let rational thought in, because I think we both know if we pause to think about this for even a second... we'll realize we shouldn't do this.

When we're naked, I kiss Ashley's neck and push my fingers inside of her, working her g-spot until she's gasping in my ear and digging her nails into my shoulders. I bring her to orgasm and as she's coming, I slip my fingers out of her and grab her clit, pinching it hard enough to make her moan turn into a shocked gasp.

Her eyes fly open and meet mine and I see the complete and utter lust in her eyes. I move my fingers away from her clit, running my hands up the back of her thighs. I grip her ass and lift her into the air.

She comes up off the ground easily and wraps her legs around me as I slip inside of her. I pump into her, hard and fast against the wall. I can't believe I once thought she was too fragile for this. She might be light, but she's anything but fragile.

The sex is fast and furious as we grope each other roughly, our kisses desperate and full of crazed passion and longing. I slam into Ashley again and again. It is almost as if I'm punishing her for making me feel jealous. When she comes, she bites down on my shoulder. I suck in a pained breath. Her teeth send shivers through me, pain and pleasure mingling in a most deliciously unexpected way.

My climax blasts through me, spreading fire through my cock, up into my stomach and out into my limbs. I come hard, spurting into Ashley's clenching pussy as she screams my name.

As her orgasm starts to recede, I hold her in place for a moment until I get myself back under control. One hand on Ashley's ass and one on the wall I steady myself. When I begin to feel normal again, I walk over to the couch with Ashley clinging to me like a little monkey. I deposit her on the couch and sit down beside her, reaching down for the blanket that's still sitting on the little table beside the couch.

I spread the blanket over us and she snuggles against me.

She smiles up at me, her cheeks flushed from the orgasm she's just had. "You know, if you're going to do that every time, I will bring strange men back here more often," she grins.

"Don't bother," I growl.

She tilts her face up at me.

I lean down and kiss her full on the mouth. I can't understand why this woman alone can turn me to mush without doing anything.

16

ASHLEY

I can't for the life of me work Finn out. Or myself.

All I know is this feels like more than just a crush in some ways, but in other ways, it feels like that's all it should be. The way we don't seem to be able to hold ourselves back from having sex with each other is mad and crazy, and it shouldn't even be legal.

In some ways, what we're doing together feels good and I think I should let it play out and see where it goes, but in other ways, in the sensible part of my head, it feels like a train wreck waiting to happen. It's funny because Finn often accuses me of thinking with my emotions rather than my head, and yet he's not exactly putting a stop to what keeps happening. I just wish he were thinking with his heart rather than his cock. And that's where the problem lies.

That's how I know I'll end up hurt.

The chemistry between Finn and me is undeniable now, but

for him, I think that's as far as it goes. Yes, that's definitely as far as it goes. He doesn't want more. I'm pretty certain he doesn't feel anything else for me except lust. If he does, he certainly doesn't show it. He instigated the sex last night and afterwards, I know he was the one who spread a blanket over us and cuddled into me. But that's how he probably is with all his women.

After all, he seems perfectly capable of having sex with me and then going back to us being a business arrangement and nothing more. I don't like the idea of us being just fuck buddies, but I also don't want to put a stop to it.

Even the thought of Finn and me being in close proximity to each other and not having sex is just unthinkable. God, why can't I be one of those women who can have sex with a hot guy and not get attached to him? Why can't I be someone who just takes pleasure in the moment and doesn't feel the need to analyze everything and overthink it?

Maybe if I move out of Finn's apartment and put some physical distance between us, I could make sense of my emotions, put it into perspective a little bit more. I should just make up with my father and ask to go back home. Or take one of those shithole apartments I've viewed until I can find somewhere better.

It'll look weird me moving out of Finn's place just three weeks away from marrying him. And besides, I don't want to move out. I like living with Finn. And that's the truth of it. I like being here. It feels right, like I'm exactly where I'm meant to be.

Even now, I've rushed home from work earlier than I usually would, to try and spend some time with Finn because I know I won't see much of him tomorrow evening. He's having dinner at his parents' place tomorrow evening. I'd been invited to the dinner, but I politely declined. Helen is so damned scary and it's more than enough when I have to see so much of her for the wedding planning, let alone socializing with her. I've only met Finn's father once. He came to the apartment and Finn introduced him to me, but I was rushing out and we never got past hello. While he seemed nice enough, it doesn't mean I want to sit through an awkward dinner with him.

Heck, I don't even know how that would go. Would we all sit around the dinner table and pretend like Finn and I are a normal couple, or would we acknowledge the fact this is a sham relationship?

I wonder what Helen would make of the fact that Finn and I can't seem to keep our hands off each other when we're alone together. I smile at the thought of her patronizing face. Would she be annoyed at Finn being with someone so socially inept?

The intercom buzzes and I frown.

At first, I think Finn has forgotten his keys, but I remember the doorman. There's no way he'd call up ahead to tell me Finn is here. Finn would obviously just come up. Unless he's making sure I'm home first, just to save himself the journey if I'm not. I'm not going to solve the mystery sitting here dithering that's for sure. I get up off the couch and move to the intercom then press the talk button. "Hello?" I say.

"Hello, Ms. Winters. I have a Janette Lake for Mr. Jagger," the doorman greets.

"Umm, okay, send her up please."

Who the hell is Janette Lake and what do I do with her? I've never heard Finn mention the name, but she could be a business associate or something. Then if Finn is on his way here to meet her while running a little bit late and I send her away, I don't imagine he'll be too happy about it.

I wait by the door until a light knock comes, then I open it.

The woman standing there is probably in her mid-thirties at a guess. She's very beautiful with long tumbling blonde curls and a full figure with curves in all the right places. She's wearing a cute little white skirt that shows her long, tanned legs, a vest top that shows her ample cleavage, and very, very high heels. In other words, she's exactly Finn's type, down to the clothes she's wearing which look very designer. "Oh," she exclaims, looking confused that I'm not Finn. Clearly, she wasn't expecting a woman to be here. She probably doesn't know Finn is engaged.

"Who are you?" she demands rudely.

"I'm Ashley," I introduce, standing back to let the woman inside. I almost add that I'm Finn's fiancée, but I remember how angry I was with Finn for doing that with Alan yesterday, and I decide to be the bigger person. Just because this woman is gorgeous doesn't mean she's not just a friend or a business associate of Finn's. And if she is a business associate, maybe he doesn't want her knowing the details of his personal life. "Finn isn't here," I say flatly. I can't help the way my voice sounds sullen and unhelpful.

"Do you know where he is?"

I shake my head. "No, I'm sorry I have no idea. I can text him and find out."

"That would be great, thank you." Janette smiles for the first time and she has amazing teeth.

She still isn't telling me why she's here, but I'm starting to think Finn must have been expecting her and got caught up at the office or something. She seems like she expected him to be here.

I go and get my phone from the counter and send Finn a quick text. *Where are you? There's a Janette Lake here to see you.* I press send and Janette and I stand and look at each other awkwardly while I wait for a response. "Why don't we sit down?" I say when the silence gets too much even for me.

Janette nods and struts over to the tall stools by the counter. She slips gracefully onto one and perches there like she belongs.

Clearing my throat, I follow her and sit down one stool away from her. My phone pings as I sit down. I open a text from Finn and read it quickly.

I'll be there in ten minutes.

It's short and to the point. I'm relieved Finn will be home soon and this awkward encounter will be over, but I'm also a little... something. I don't know, angry maybe? That he's dropping everything and rushing over to see Janette. I remind myself this is most likely business. Maybe she was meant to meet him at the office and got her wires crossed or something. But something about the way she is dressed and looks tells me she has nothing to do with business. "Finn's on his way home. He'll be here in ten minutes," I tell her shortly.

"Oh, thank God," Janette remarks with a short laugh. "I know you're going to think this is ridiculous, but I left an earring in his car last night, and I really have to get it back. I know it's only an earring, but it has sentimental value to me, and I haven't been able to settle since I realized I lost it. I'm just glad I worked out where it must be."

I smile and nod, but I'm not really listening to Janette's silky voice and her perfect laugh. I'm seething inside. There's only one way a person loses her earring in a car and doesn't notice immediately... the thought of Finn and Janette fucking, then him coming home and fucking me turns my stomach. I actually want to vomit on her. "I completely get it," I mutter when I realize Janette is waiting for me to say something.

I get it all right. It's a good excuse to come back for round two. "I'm sorry, but I have some work calls I need to make. Would you excuse me?"

"Oh, yes of course," Janette replies sweetly. "I'm so sorry to have disturbed you."

"It's fine," I reply with a fake smile as I stand up. "Hope you find your earring."

"Thanks," Janette replies.

I walk towards the hallway so I can escape to my bedroom. I'm glad I wasn't rude to Janette. I mean it's not her fault

Finn's been fucking us both. And it's not like he's really done anything wrong, at least not to me. I don't know what kind of arrangement he and Janette have, and I don't want to know, but our own deal was clear. We can sleep with whomever we like as long as we don't humiliate each other in public.

In other words, this is my problem, my issue. And as much as it hurts me, I can't allow myself to say anything to Finn about this. And certainly, not to Janette.

I sit on my bed for a moment, unsure what to do with myself now that I've left the room. My insides are churning, and whether I like it or not, I have to admit to myself, I am insanely jealous of this woman, of the idea of sharing Finn with her. Maybe it would be easier if she wasn't so stunningly beautiful, but no, that's not it. I don't want to share Finn with anyone. I want him to be as consumed with me as I have become with him.

I try to let go of the jealousy, but I just can't. I keep picturing Finn kissing Janette, her hands on him, his on her. And I can see more images of the two of them, more scenarios I most definitely don't want to even imagine.

I feel like crying.

I feel like going out there and clawing Janette's blue eyes out. Of course, I do neither. Instead, I just sit here, staring straight ahead of me, trying to make the mental images of Finn and Janette go away, holding back the tears of fury and hurt.

I hear the front door opening and bile fills my throat,

burning it, as I imagine Finn kissing Janette hello. I hear their voices fill the air. I can't make out the words, only the cadence of their voices. Finn doesn't sound angry or anything. Dammit. In the fantasy, I had in my head I wanted him to be angry, to come storming in here and tell me he's never met this woman in his life and why have I allowed her into his apartment.

They talk a little more and then the apartment door opens and closes again. I breathe a momentary sigh of relief that Janette has gone, then I steel myself to see Finn again. I wait, but he doesn't come to my room. Why would he? He knows he hasn't broken any of our rules and he doesn't know I'm letting myself get attached to him. He doesn't think he has anything to apologize for.

He really doesn't have to apologize and that's the worst part of it all.

Why didn't I make the rule be that we were to be exclusive while this whole damned wedding thing was hanging over our heads? The answer to that one is obvious. I thought I hated Finn. I didn't care who he slept with or what he did. Now, this has changed and come back to bite me in the ass.

I stand up restlessly. I'm not going to hide here like some little coward. I'm going to go out there and face him. I'm not going to yell or accuse him of anything, I'm just going to go and get a glass of water so we can get this over with. I have to look at him and know if anything has changed in his mind as it is starting to change in mine. Maybe this will be the kick in the ass I need to remind myself of why I can't let myself fall for Finn. Not even a little bit.

I slip out of the bedroom and make my way along the hallway, my head held high, my shoulders back, every muscle in my neck and shoulders tense. I step into the living room, but it's empty. Finn's jacket isn't here. I reach up and rub the tight spot on my neck.

"Finn?" I call.

I am rewarded only with silence.

Suddenly, I'm not so pleased that Janette has left the apartment, because Finn has actually gone with her.

I am horrified to feel tears prickling at the corners of my eyes. I turn around and practically run back to my bedroom. I throw myself on the bed and let the tears come. They are hot and salty and I feel like they burn paths of shame down my cheeks.

I indulge myself in my own pity party for a couple of minutes and then I tell myself not to be so ridiculous. I came into this with my eyes wide open and I knew Finn and I would be going our separate ways at the end of it.

It is the only sensible outcome for both of us.

I get up off the bed and go to the bathroom. I run a bubble bath and spend a long time soaking in it, trying to read my book. I tell myself I'm not going to even think about Finn, but my ears are pricked for any sound of him returning.

By the time I hear him come in, I'm already in bed.

It's late. Like late, late. And although I tell myself I don't care at all, I feel my heart aching as I imagine what he and Janette have spent the night doing.

When I finally fall asleep, it's a fitful sleep, full of dark nightmares where I see Finn. He smiles and opens his arms, and as I go to run into them, Janette runs up from behind me, overtakes me, and gets there first. I realize his arms were never open for me in the first place.

The invitation was always for her only.

17

FINN

Dinner with my parents is strange to say the least. My mom was full of talk of the wedding and how the plans are coming along. She gushed about Ashley's dress, the flowers for the hall and the beautiful grounds where the reception was to be held, as if it were real. She truly sounded like she almost believes this is real. My father stayed quiet about the whole thing, just blending into the background and letting my mom chatter on.

Perhaps the weirdest thing about it all was that throughout the meal, all I could think of was Ashley. At first, I wished she was here with me, a buffer to take some of the attention away from me for a while, but then I remembered her reaction when I invited her to come and have dinner with us, and I realized I wouldn't wish that on her.

As the night drones on, I start to wish I were back home with her.

The food is delicious, catered by a famous chef that my

mom uses, but I would have swapped it for Chinese food from the carton if it meant I get to spend the night with Ashley instead of being here.

I'd gotten home late last night and missed her, and then this morning, she'd already left when I got up. It scared me a little to see I'd missed her that much, and I tried to tell myself it was just because she was the lesser of two evils, her company more appealing than my mom's wedding talk, but I know it is more than that though.

I am relieved when my father suggests we go and finish our drinks in the living room. It's my cue to drink up and stand. It felt too rude to excuse myself from the dinner table and rush off. I mean it's barely nine o'clock. But doing so from the living room is more acceptable.

We move to the living room and sit down.

"How's work going Finn?" My father asks me.

"Good," I say, nodding. "It's crazy busy, but that's the intention so I'm pleased about it. Even the board has backed off a little bit. I think they're finally starting to see that maybe I do know what I'm doing after all. It's been a long hard road to get to this point, but now the systems are all in place and the profit is starting to come in."

"You're not going to cancel the wedding, are you?" My mom interrupts before my dad can respond.

"What? No, of course not. Why would I?" I ask.

"Well, aren't you marrying Ashley so the board can't over-rule you on this? It sounds like maybe they wouldn't even try to now." My mom looks like she is about to have a heart attack on the spot at the thought of the shame of a wedding being called off.

My father clears his throat and shifts uncomfortably on the couch. "Despite the fact your mother here thinks she's planning a royal wedding and that it's become the single focus of her life, if you want to call it off Finn, don't feel like you can't do that."

"I'm marrying Ashley so I retain control of what I have built. And even if the board comes around to this, there will be more difficult decisions to make down the line, and they'll continue to oppose anything that doesn't fit their 1970s way of looking at things so I'm not calling anything off," I say gently, then quickly move the conversation onto safer ground, "How's work going for you Dad?"

"Not bad. Actually, I was talking to a man a couple of days ago who I recommended your firm to. His details are in the safe in my office. Would you go and grab the file and we'll go over it together?"

"Sure," I say, relieved to be given an excuse to get away from my parents for a moment, now that the inevitable fight about the wedding is already brewing.

My mom has been giving my dad the death stare since he suggested it would be okay to cancel the wedding. I think in my mom's eyes, the only acceptable way for that to happen would be if either Ashley or I dropped dead. Maybe not even then.

I hurry from the room and go to my dad's office. I move to the large painting on the wall and take it down, shaking my head at my dad's clichéd way of hiding his safe. Like this wouldn't be the first place a thief looked.

I enter the combination; my birthday and my mom's birthday, another easy guess for any thief who'd bothered to do a bit of research before breaking into the house, and wait for the door to click open. There's a large brown envelope propped up right at the front of the safe and I go to push it to one side, but the name on it catches my eye.

Arthur Jagger. Last will and testament.

I shake my head. It's like I can't escape my grandpa's legacy for even a second. My breath catches in my throat when I spot the date on the envelope. It's dated three months after the document Andrew Garfield presented to us. With a shaking hand, I reach into the safe and pull the envelope out.

There has to be something bad in here for my dad to be hiding it from me and my mom. What other crazy stipulations has my grandpa added to his will? And doesn't my dad know that if they're not met and this document ever reaches the light of day, I'll lose everything? If it's as bad as I'm imagining, he should have just shredded it, as Andrew clearly doesn't know of its existence.

As I start to pull out the papers from the envelope, I realize that it might not affect me. Maybe the bits that have changed since the other will are about something else and that's why I haven't seen this document. Perhaps it just references the original document for my part of the legacy and that's why Andrew was using the old will.

I scan through the part about me quickly and then I reread

it slowly, sure I've missed something. I haven't. I know I haven't, but I read it a third time just to be sure. I'm right. I shake my head and flick through the rest of the document, giving it nothing but a cursory glance. Nothing else has changed.

As I flick through the papers, a sheet of paper with my grandpa's handwriting on it falls to the ground. I pick it up and read it and it confirms everything I have just read. It's a short letter from my grandpa to my father.

Dearest Gerald,

If you are reading this letter, then I am no more.

I hope you're okay with that for I have lived a full and active life, and I am okay with it coming to an end and you should be too. Live your life, son, and don't waste any time worrying about me.

My attorney is under strict instructions to deliver this to you exactly one week after the reading of my will. He has no idea what's inside of it. As you've no doubt worked out, it's a new and updated version of my last will and testament. It's been officially written and is above board, and once it is brought forward, it will replace my old will. You can bring it to Garfield's attention if you so desire.

The only change is as follows: in the event of my death, my grandson, Finn Jagger, will inherit my shares in my company in their entirety. Contrary to my first will and testament, Finn does not have to marry Ashley Winters nor anyone else, to gain his inheritance.

I suppose you could say I've gone soft, because as I wrote out my first will, my chief concern was bringing the two families, that of me and Walter Winters, back together. I thought if our grandchildren were brought together, it could make for a great partnership. In time, I've come to see that forcing Finn and Ashley onto each other is wrong.

I do hope that by the time this letter and will come to light they will have at the very least developed a firm friendship, and I hope they can laugh about this.

Please give this will to Finn when you feel the time is right.

Your loving father,

Arthur J Jagger

At least, now I know why my father was adamant I could cancel the wedding if I wanted to. And he's clearly left this here for me to find. I should be overjoyed. I don't have to go through with any of this now, and I actually think my grandpa was right about one thing. I really think when I tell Ashley about this, we'll both laugh. It'll be a relieved laugh, but we'll laugh all the same. And I think he might be right about us being friends now.

Funny thing is, I can't imagine not having Ashley in my life anymore. I can't imagine going back to my apartment knowing she will never be there.

I think of my mom. This is going to destroy her. Cancelling the wedding will seem like such a bigger deal to her than a divorce would. That's how her society friends work. A divorce is almost expected, but a cancelled wedding?

Well, that's a scandal.

I can't think too much about this now. My head is spinning. I push the papers and the letter back into the envelope and push it to the back of the safe, leaving a message for my father telling him I've seen the will. I grab the file he sent me to get, as that was clearly a ruse to let me see the letter without my mother knowing about it.

My plan is to go through this file then get the hell out of here and talk to Ashley about this. Bring her the good news that we no longer have to marry each other. But why doesn't it feel like good news, dammit? It must be the shock. Yes, that's all it is. It's not like I wanted to marry her, so I should be relieved. And she will be too.

By the time I close the safe and return to the living room, I'm composed and hopefully I look normal again.

"Ah, you found it?" my father says.

He's looking at the file in my hand, but I know his question is about something else... the will.

I nod once. "Yes, I did." I sit down beside him on the couch. "Now who's this client?"

He looks at me out of the corner of his eye and I know he's dying for a signal as to what I think of the letter. I think he expected me to march in here with the will in my hand and announce that the wedding is off. Yes, that's it. Then he could claim he had forgotten about the will, say he was trying to hide it from me so the shame of a cancelled wedding isn't on him. I don't blame him. My mother is not exactly easy. I can walk away, but he has to live here with her.

When he sees he's not getting his circus, he takes the file from me and opens it up.

I spot the name on the top. "Ah him. It's okay, Dad. He's already called me. We're going to be doing business together. Thank you for sending him my way."

"Anytime, son. You know I'll always have your back, right?"

"Right." I stand up quickly, suddenly afraid my mom will leave the room, and I'll be left to answer questions I'm not ready to. "Well, thank you for a lovely evening, and a great dinner, Mom. I'm sorry to rush off like this, but I have things I need to take care of."

I see relief on my father's face. He's confident that by the end of tonight, the wedding will be called off. I'm sure once I've spoken to Ashley about it, I'll be as relieved as my dad is. I'll still give everything I promised to Ashley.

My mom stands up and hugs me. "Remind Ashley we have another dress fitting to attend tomorrow."

"I will," I promise, although it's not actually going to happen now.

I say my goodbyes, hurry out to my waiting car, and head back to my apartment. I try not to think about any of the letter or what it means to Ashley and me. At least now, I know why the condition was there at all. My grandpa just wanted to bring Ashley and me together, to maybe have us form a bond like him and Walter did all of those years ago. That makes sense in a nostalgic sort of a way. And he did do that. I feel very protective and close to Ashley.

I step into the apartment. Ashley is sitting in her pajamas on the ground, files and papers spread all around her. An untouched glass of wine sits on the coffee table.

"What are you doing?" I ask as I step inside and close the door behind me.

"Oh, I'm sorry. I wasn't expecting you yet. I'll clear all of this mess away and go and try to fathom it out in my room," she says, reaching for the files.

She looks stressed out and I can hear the shaky quality in her voice that tells me she's close to tears. "Don't be silly. I'm not complaining about you working here. I just wondered what you were doing." I go and sit down on the floor beside her.

She sighs loudly. "My assistant quit and I haven't been able to replace her yet. And I have all of these things to sort out and I don't know where to start with most of them," she says in a rush. "There are bills outstanding, and meetings to rearrange, and in amongst all of that, I have to find a way to still run the foodbank and deal with the donations."

"Okay, take a deep breath first," I tell her.

"That's easy for you to say. You're not the one on the verge of losing everything." She sighs. "I'm sorry. I don't mean to sound so dramatic. I'll find a way through all of this, just like I've always done. But right now, it just feels impossible."

"What do you need?" I ask.

"To not lose anything else."

"Be more specific, Ashley. Right now, in this moment, what would help you sort this mess out?"

"An assistant who's qualified and can take over someone else's mess and sift through it without dropping any balls." She smiles at me, a weary smile. "A unicorn in other words."

"Well, I don't have a unicorn as such but I do have a team of assistants. I'll call Tyson and see which would be the best placed to work in the charity sector and you can borrow them for a month or two until you find someone, or have them train a new person."

She shakes her head.

I raise an eyebrow. Surely, she's not too proud to borrow a member of my staff if it means keeping her charity afloat?

"I appreciate the offer Finn, really I do, but the charity can't afford to pay the kind of salary a company like yours pays, and no one is going to come and work for me for less money."

I see the problem and I know exactly how to deal with it in a way she won't see as me taking pity on her. "Oh, no you don't. I see what you're doing and it's not going to happen."

"Huh?"

"Trying to get them off my payroll and onto yours so you can keep them? I don't think so, Ashley. It's a loan of a member of staff, nothing more than that," I tell her. "I'll be paying their salary and while they will be at your beck and call for the time you need them, there's a two-month limit on that." I pause and shake my head. "I can't believe I made a nice gesture and you saw an opportunity to poach someone from my staff."

"That's not what I meant," she corrects.

"A likely story," I reply. "Now, do you want me to make the call on my terms or not?"

She nods slowly.

I stand up and start to head to my office to make the call.

As I cross the room, Ashley calls out from behind me, "Finn?"

I turn back.

She smiles at me. "I know what you're doing... and why you're doing it. Thank you."

I smile back at her, afraid that if I confirm what she's thinking, she'll change her mind. I go to my office and call Tyson. I explain to him what I need and he recommends Andrea, a young and ambitious team member who came to us from a nonprofit company which she left when she saw there was no path for betterment there for her. I tell Tyson to call her and have her meet Ashley at her office at eight in the morning, and to make it clear to Andrea that this is a personal favor to me and not a demotion, or a way of getting her out of the back door.

Tyson texts me within five minutes, saying it's all sorted and Andrea will be there.

I go back to the living room.

Ashley looks up as I walk towards her.

I shake my head, my face grave. "I'm sorry Ashley. We won't be able to give you a unicorn."

Her face drops.

"But..." I pause dramatically, "...we will however be giving you Andrea, a professional assistant with experience working in the nonprofit sector."

"Oh, you bastard," Ashley breathes with a grin.

I laugh. "I think the words you're looking for are thank you, but whatever."

"Seriously, you almost gave me heart failure there. But yes, thank you. You have no idea what this means to me, Finn."

I sit back down beside her and smile at her. "It's my pleasure. Now, what else do you need?"

"Nothing," she says, smiling again. "Really, that's just taken a huge weight off my mind. When will I meet her?"

"She's meeting you at your office at eight o'clock tomorrow morning. After that, you can set her hours to suit you both."

"That's good," Ashley chimes, staring off into the distance for a moment. "That'll give me enough time to go over everything with her and get her set up before I have to meet your mom for a dress fitting."

"About that..." I start.

"Oh, God what now? Finn I can't cope with anything else changing right now," she grumbles.

"It's nothing. My mom just asked me to remind you about it, that's all."

Now isn't the time to talk about the new will. If she hears the words "the wedding's off" she's actually going to hear the words "the deal is off" right now. And in the frazzled state she's in, I'd never get her to hear me when I tell her that I'm still going to be donating the money as we discussed it. She isn't the one who broke the deal and her charity shouldn't suffer because of it. Hell, I'm actually happy to be giving her this money. My grandpa's moment of nostalgia has already caused enough upheaval as it is.

I decide to tell her tomorrow evening when she has Andrea all settled in and working her magic, when she's a little less stressed. She'll understand why I chose to wait a day and she'll be so relieved that she doesn't have to marry me, she won't care too much about waiting an extra day to find out about it.

Ashley is rubbing at that spot on her neck again, the one that seems to tense up.

I already know whenever she gets herself stressed out like this, she does the same thing. "Here, let me," I say, reaching up and rubbing the knot.

I didn't think it through before I said it, but Ashley accepts my touch without complaint. She's either so stressed out she just wants this knot gone any way she can get it to happen, or like me, she knows where this will end up and she's inviting it. But now I know what I know, can I still go through with that?

Sure, I can, I tell myself. It'll be the perfect way for us to say goodbye. And it's not like the sex is in anyway part of the deal. It's something I think Ashley would still want to do even if she knew we don't have to get married anymore. Especially, since she thinks weddings are unnecessary. Who knows, knowing this would probably turn her on even more. Still, I'm cautious, barely touching her, just moving the tips of my fingers over the knot.

Ashley turns to the side and leans back slightly, giving me easier access.

I realize she's felt the fact I am barely touching her, and put it down to the awkward angle. I begin to massage her more deeply, and sure enough, within moments, she's moaning and my cock is hard.

I know she feels it at the base of her spine. She's sitting between my legs, her ass pressed against it. There's no way she cannot be feeling it. She doesn't comment though and I keep massaging her, trying to ignore the way I feel inside, like I just want to fuck her all night long.

She starts to unbutton her pajama top and I push my hands inside of it, moving them over the tops of her shoulders. I start to move my hands lower and soon, I'm massaging the top of her breasts.

Ashley sighs, a contented sigh that tells me she's thoroughly enjoying this.

I lean forward and kiss her neck and she moans again, leaning her body back against mine. I run my tongue down her neck and over the top of her shoulder, my hands now massaging her breasts fully. I can feel her nipples rubbing against my palms, hardening at my touch. The skin around them is puckered with goose bumps.

I kiss back up along her neck and suck her ear lobe into my mouth.

She gasps, but this time, it's not with pleasure then she springs away from me.

For a horrible second, I think I've somehow hurt her.

She begins to gather up her files, doing it so fast that loose papers flutter from some of them.

I automatically start to help her. "Are you all right?" I ask. "Did I hurt you?"

"I'm fine. And no, you didn't. I just... I just have to get these files put away," she mutters as she jumps to her feet. She holds her hand out for the papers I'm holding.

I debate holding them hostage until she tells me what's wrong, but I decide against it and just give them to her. She's not going to want to open up to me if she feels like I'm forcing her to talk to me.

Then she rushes out of the living room, not even looking back.

I hear her bedroom door closing and rub my hand over my own neck. I close my eyes for a moment. I don't know what the hell went wrong there, but it wasn't anything to do with her needing to start collecting up those files.

I stand up and move towards the hallway. I'm not going to push this. If Ashley doesn't want to have sex with me, then all she has to do is say so, but I'm not going to let her run off like that without talking to me, not when something is clearly bothering her.

I don't bother knocking on her door. Something tells me she

wouldn't respond if I did, and it's not like she's been gone long enough to be naked or anything. I step into the room.

Ashley is perched on the end of the bed and she glares at me when I come in.

"Ashley, what's wrong?"

"Nothing," she says.

"Well, you need to tell your face nothing is wrong, because if looks could kill, I'd be dead right now."

She shrugs and turns her head to look out of the window.

Dammit, this woman is frustrating. "Look, clearly there is something wrong and if you don't want anything to happen between us, then fine, it won't. But I'm not a damned mind reader Ashley, and if something is bothering you, then you need to tell me what it is."

"Why do I need to tell you what it is? It's not like we're married yet and you can order me around."

"I'm pretty sure this isn't the Victorian times and even if it were, I can't even imagine ordering you, of all people around," I joke, trying to lighten the mood.

It doesn't work. Ashley just keeps staring at the window.

I sigh loudly. "Well, if I've upset you somehow, I'm sorry. But we both know the apology would be a little more genuine if I knew what I was actually apologizing for."

Ashley finally turns to look at me. She doesn't look angry. She looks resigned, like she knows she has to say this, but she really doesn't want to. "Fine, I'll tell you. Things between us, they got a little complicated, didn't they? And that's not what either of us wanted. I'm not blaming you Finn, and you don't owe me an apology. This is my issue not yours, so I'll find a way to get over it. We talked and we both agreed we could see whomever we wanted to, and that's okay. I'm not angry. But I don't want to be just another one of your women."

"I don't understand." I'm genuinely confused as to what the hell she's talking about. She's making it sound like I'm suddenly fucking half of the women in the city or something.

"I thought I was okay with this being meaningless sex between us, but I'm not. I can't cope with the thought of you fucking her and then coming home and fucking me. I'm sorry if you think that makes me petty, but that's the way it's got to be. Do you understand?"

"I understand the sentiment, but I've got no idea where this is coming from, or who this 'her' you're talking about is."

"Janette, of course," Ashley spits.

I move to the bed and sit down beside Ashley. She stiffens slightly but she doesn't move away and I take that as a good sign. "Where did this come from? Because I'm *not* sleeping with Janette. Hell, I haven't properly dated anyone in years. Work just got in the way of all of that stuff. I never met anyone special enough for me to leave the office early for, and as you can imagine, any girl I did try to date got pretty pissed off about me cancelling on them for work stuff all the time. So in the end, I just stopped bothering. I've had a few one night stands, but the last one was months before I met you," I admit honestly.

"And you expect me to believe that?" Ashley asks quietly.

"Honestly Ashley, I don't much care one way or the other. It's the truth and you can choose to believe it or you can choose to be a cynic and assume the worst of me. I'm not going to beg you to believe me, because as you say, our deal didn't prohibit me from doing what I wanted with other women so I have no reason to lie to you, or beg you to believe me."

Ashley goes quiet for a moment while she thinks this through. "I want to believe you, Finn. But it's kind of hard after yesterday. Girls don't lose their earrings in cars unless they've been fucking in them," she remarked.

"Nice way of putting it." I grin. "And you're right. Janette did lose her earring while fucking in the car, but it wasn't me she was fucking. She's Lester's wife."

"Who is Lester?" Ashley asks.

"One of my drivers," I explain. "She came for the earring herself because Lester refused to ask me. He assumed he would be fired when I worked out how Janette lost an earring in the backseat of my car."

"Why didn't he just get it himself and not involve you at all?" Ashley asked.

"Because I had already found it. I knew it must be hers, but he refused to admit it was Janette's. I was waiting for him to own up. I rate honestly very highly in my staff. I had it in the office safe, so I took her back to the office and gave it to her."

"You were gone so long though," Ashley points out.

"Yeah, I wasn't finished working. Next time I need to work late, I'll be sure to ask your permission," I point out, getting a little tired of having to explain myself.

"God, I'm sorry, Finn. I'm such an idiot," Ashley said, shaking her head. "I should just have talked to you about it. Or better yet, just minded my own damn business."

"Let's face it, I didn't exactly handle Alan any better than you handled Lester's wife," I admit.

She laughs softly. "I guess we're both much too stubborn to just actually ask the hard questions."

"Or maybe we were both afraid of the answers."

"You know, for a guy who doesn't date, you seem to have all of the right answers," she remarks softly.

"I don't cook, but I still know when a burger tastes good," I point out.

She bursts out laughing and I join her. Her laugh is infectious and I know for sure now that I am in real trouble here. I explained myself because I wanted Ashley to know I didn't sleep with anyone else. Because I wanted her to know, she's become special to me. "Listen, Ashley," I say when our laughter dies down.

She turns to face me, seeming to sense what I'm about to say is serious.

"I know we agreed not to complicate this, but it seems like it's a little late for that. If you don't want me to touch you anymore, I get it, and I swear I won't. I'll find a way to think of you as a friend and nothing more, but I want to be with you. I like the complications." I smile at her.

She smiles back.

"I guess what I'm trying to say is... I don't want to stop whatever it is we've started here. And—" I don't get a chance to finish because Ashley's mouth is suddenly on mine. She kisses me and I kiss her back, our arms going around each other.

"And...?" She prompts, pulling back from my kiss for a moment, a twinkle in her eyes.

"And... oh, who cares. I just really want to kiss you again."

"I'm agreeable to that," she beams as she leans closer to me again.

I kiss her, pushing my tongue into her mouth, tasting her lips, her teeth, her tongue. As I kiss her, I start to open the buttons on her pajama top. I get them open and push her top down her arms, my hands skimming over her back then down her sides before coming around to the front of her body and massaging her breasts. I want to feel every inch of her skin, taste every part of it.

Ashley tugs at my shirt and I take my hands off her breasts and my mouth off her lips, long enough for her to rip my shirt off then throw it to the ground. We come back together, our mouths seeking each other out. I stand, pulling her up with me and her hands go to my jeans, opening them and pushing them down. She comes back for my boxer shorts and pushes them down too. I kick my shoes off and follow them with my jeans and boxers and then I step back from Ashley.

"Tonight is all about you," I say, my voice husky.

She reaches out for me, but I sidestep her grasping arms and grab her. I push her gently onto the bed. She lands on her bottom and I motion for her to scoot backwards. She does as I direct her. I lean down and grasp her pajama bottoms by the ankles. She lifts her ass and I yank them off her. She's not wearing any underwear and I feel heat flood me at the sight of her laying there naked, open, and mine for the taking.

I want to pounce on her and enter her, but I hold myself back. Tonight is all about her and I meant it. I want to make her come before I enter her. I crawl onto the bed and lift Ashley's right leg. I kiss her ankle and then make my way up her calf, moving slowly up her lower leg in a trail of kisses. I move my mouth gently over her knee, running my tongue up her thigh, stopping when I get to her pussy. I take a deep breath, breathing in the sweet scent of Ashley's pussy. I pick up her left leg and kiss my way up that one too.

I lick over her inner thighs, and see goosebumps rush over the surface of her skin. Then I push her legs wide apart and stare down at all that beauty. All that lovely, wet flesh. All mine. I move closer to her and run my tongue over the outside of her pink lips until she's begging me to move to her clit, to end the teasing touches. I smile to myself as I kiss along her quivering flesh, until finally, I give her what she wants and begin to lap at her clit.

She moans beneath me as I suck her clit into my mouth,

pressing it against the ridges on the top of my mouth. Her moans become longer when I gently vibrate my tongue, making rippling motions over her clit. Finally, I release my hold on her and begin to lick her gently.

I push two fingers into her pussy, finding her g-spot. I work it in time with my tongue. I up my pace, licking her harder and harder... within moments, she's coming hard. Her pussy squirting liquid into my mouth and running down my chin to the duvet as her eyes roll back in her head, her whole body tenses as she drops over the edge of the abyss of pleasure.

I pull my fingers out of her pussy and lick down her slit. I lick around the edge of her pussy. She moans with an almost pained sound as I thrust my tongue inside of her while my fingers continue to work her clit, hard and fast. Within seconds, she's coming again... and again, I greedily drink up her juices, relishing the taste of her on my tongue.

I keep working her until her moans trail off to gasping breaths, until her legs have come up and wrapped themselves around my shoulders as her hands become like claws at her sides.

Finally, I come up for air and I gently push her legs away from my shoulders. They fall to the mattress, floppy and pliable. Her pussy is still open, but it now looks swollen and red. I have to force myself not to suck it anymore, because I know it must be tender by now.

Gently, I kiss Ashley's stomach and move up to her breasts. I suck one of her nipples into my mouth and work the other one between my fingertips. Ashley's nipples are as hard as rocks and I know how sensitive they are by the way she writhes beneath me, small whimpers escaping her mouth as I tease her.

I kiss up along her chest and run my tongue up her throat until my mouth is locked on hers. She reaches down and puts her hands on my ass, pulling my body tighter against hers. I push into her, feeling her warm, wet pussy opening up for me.

I began to move, but instead of pounding into Ashley, I move slowly, filling her up with slow, sensual strokes that make her cling to me and whisper my name. I keep kissing her as I move inside of her, our tongues entwining as her hips move with mine. Her hands roam over my back, holding me to her.

I feel her pussy clenching around my cock, gripping me like a glove and sending fire through my body as she comes again and again. She presses her face against my shoulder and calls my name in a strangled, broken voice as liquid douses me. I up my pace, not able to hold myself back any longer. I can feel the fire in me spreading out, warming my body as pleasure explodes through me and I spurt into Ashley.

She breathlessly whispers my name again as I remain inside and kiss her on the mouth. The kiss goes on and on, until I cannot tell where I end and she begins. Eventually, when I roll off her, she scoots towards me and snuggles against me. I kiss the top of her head, breathing in the scent of her hair.

I hold her until she falls asleep in my arms.

I smile down at her and I know then I never want to let her

go. This didn't feel like an end, it felt like a beginning. I admit to myself, lying here in the darkness listening to Ashley's gentle breathing, that I haven't just fucked her. I've made love to her. It wasn't the perfect way to say goodbye.

It was the perfect way to claim her as mine. And only mine.

All at once, I know I can't tell her about the document I found, because the thought of her walking away from me is just too much. I will tell her at some point; of course, I will. I just have to make sure she feels the same way about me first. That she's not going to take this as her cue to leave me behind and get back to her old life, a life that doesn't include me.

18

ASHLEY

The days are flying by. It's Friday and Finn and I are getting married next Saturday. The time has really whizzed by and I can't believe I'm getting married in a little over a week. It's especially crazy, considering I didn't even know Finn this time last month.

The time has gone by filled with dress fittings, tasting menus, and a hundred other wedding details. I have spent a lot of time with Helen who doesn't seem as scary anymore, although I still wouldn't like to think I made a wrong choice for something and somehow angered her. All the details I consider minor seem so terribly important to her. I've even allowed her to plan my hairstyle. The hairstylist is going to sweep my hair together with some hair extensions and put it into a loose bun at the nape of my neck. I suppose it will look nice.

I've had my final dress fitting today and I have to say it's a beautiful dress and while it's way more expensive than anything I normally would have chosen I can't wait to wear it. It actually has a rather magical effect on me. It makes me feel like a fairy tale princess when I'm in it. Maybe Finn's ideas on marriage are rubbing off on me, because you don't have to wear a pretty dress just to sign a contract.

Pretty much all of the plans are in place for the wedding now, and the few bits that still need to be done are all in Damon's hands. The RSVPs are all in and it's on Damon to work out the numbers, make sure the right amount of meals and drinks are ordered, the wedding favors are all put together then delivered. And on the day, all I have to worry about is getting ready, with help from the professionals Helen has hired, of course. Damon will worry about everything else. I guess I can sort of understand the point of a wedding planner now. With so much going on, I would be a complete wreck right now if all of the responsibility were on my shoulders.

I finally got around to telling my parents that I'm engaged and they were so thrilled I instantly felt guilty I hadn't told them the full story. It even helped to mend the argument my father and I had and led to him apologizing to me. I think they're just relieved that I have something to focus on other than the charity.

Oh well, at least their joy at me having something more traditional going on in my life stopped them from asking a thousand and one awkward questions about why we're moving so quickly with all of this and why Finn's parents are happy to pay for everything. They probably think I'm pregnant or something.

Although I really wanted to tell them the truth about the marriage, I knew I couldn't. The bridges my father and I have mended would be well and truly burned without any hope of fixing them if my parents found out my wedding is just a sham to get money for the charity. And here's the thing... I don't want to tell them and not just because of how disappointed they'll be. I don't want to tell them because in my heart, it no longer feels true. It's not a sham.

What Finn and I have is beautiful.

I know logically that nothing has changed. Finn and I will still divorce down the road, but it feels different now. Both my best friends think I'm setting myself up to get hurt, but Finn and I have talked, and it seems like I'm not the only one who is starting to think this could be something more than a fake marriage.

Finn has cautiously admitted to me that he thinks of me as more than just a friend. The whole time he said it he kept staring at me warily as if I was going to jump up and bite him. I've admitted the same thing to him, but we've agreed to take it easy. That we're not going to make a big deal out of it. We're just going to take things one day at a time, but this feels special.

Finn doesn't work late anymore unless he really can't avoid it. And I spend more time thinking about Finn than I do about the charity which is a huge, big deal for me. Not because I've lost interest in the charity, but with Andrea there and enough money to do all the things we want, there is no longer a terrible stress of not knowing whether we'll be around in the coming months.

We eat breakfast together every day ever since that night we had our heart to heart about Janette. He told me she's his driver's wife, which had been a huge relief. God, I wanted to eat him that night when he told me he wasn't sleeping with her. Talking of food, he even buys food to have at home. Yogurt, fruit, eggs, bacon, and cereal for our breakfasts together... it's a start.

We also make an effort to eat dinner together every night and we're just enjoying the closeness between us. I haven't slept in the guest bedroom since the last time Finn and I were together in there. It's not even something we discuss now. We just go to bed together in Finn's room and make love before falling asleep in each other's arms.

It's definitely more than just physical between us now though. The more time we spend together and get to know each other better, the more we see that we have so much in common. We haven't come together the conventional way, but Arthur certainly made the right choice by forcing us to come together.

We talk about Finn's business and my charity, and while we work in very different sectors, we both have the same fire, the same drive to succeed. We talk about our hopes and dreams for the future and they mostly align with each other, which is good because on most levels now, whenever I let myself think of the future, I see Finn beside me.

It's fast becoming clear to me that I massively misjudged Finn. He was never the enemy. He's not the person I thought he was at all. He's ambitious, but ethical. He's warm, kind and generous. He can make me laugh, even after days where everything has gone horribly wrong and I'm sure no one could make me laugh.

I think as Finn gets to know me, he's realizing he'd misjudged me too. Or maybe it's more a case of him learning to like the things he assumed he would hate about me, like how I am passionate and make decisions with my heart and not just my head. Like how I react to things emotionally, and if I see someone being wronged, I will attempt to fix the situation, even when doing so isn't technically my problem to fix.

"Ash? Are you almost ready? The car will be here soon," Finn calls from the living room, pulling me out of my head.

"Almost," I call back. I stand in front of the mirror, tweak my hair one last time, and smile to myself, happy with the way I look. We're going to a party tonight, one I would normally have dreaded, but I'm actually looking forward to it.

It's a yearly party being thrown by his father's oldest friend. He normally attends, but he said he knew how much I hated these things, and since it would look weird him going without me, he would get us out of it, but I shook my head and told him we should go.

I think he was more than a little shocked, but was also a little pleased. It wouldn't look good for us to hide ourselves away, and tonight is a good chance for Finn's friends and relatives to see that we're the real deal.

He gave me his credit card and told me to buy something to wear. Naturally, I started to object, accusing him of being pretentious. He laughed and told me I could shop in a thrift store if I wanted to, but he didn't think I'd want to go in my work clothes and my pajamas weren't the right shade of pink for a party. I found myself laughing with him and accepting his offer, remembering how I had felt when I was dressed all wrong for the restaurant the first day I met Helen.

I hadn't gone to a thrift shop, but I hadn't gone to an expensive designer shop either. I settled for something in the middle, going for something right for the occasion without having to feel guilty for having the dress.

"Seriously Ashley, the car is here," Finn shouts from the living room.

I can imagine him pacing, looking at his watch while wishing I'd hurry up and finish getting ready. "Coming," I shout back.

I quickly spray some perfume behind my ears and over my head. I step out of the bedroom and move quickly towards the living room.

Finn's eyes open wide when he sees me. His throat moves as he swallows hard.

"What's wrong? Is it too much?" I ask, instantly regretting the dress.

"No, it's perfect. You're perfect.". He looks at me as if he can't take his eyes off me. He smiles slowly, possessively. "You look beautiful, Ashley. There's not going to be a man there who won't envy me."

"Thank you," I say, feeling myself blushing and no longer regretting the dress. "You look great too."

And he does.

Dressed in a full suit and a tie, Finn looks dashingly handsome. For a split-second, I have to admit I am tempted to suggest we skip the party to just stay home and make love all night long, but Finn holds his arm out to me. I slip my hand through his elbow, deciding we should go to the party after all. He will look this good even after we return from the party and we can still make love all night long.

My hand tingles where it touches Finn's arm, even through his suit jacket, he has this effect on me. As he leads me from the apartment, I'm a little bit surprised to find I have butter-flies in my tummy.

19

FINN

I can hardly stop myself from staring at Ashley. We've been at the party for almost two hours now, and I'm still as completely enchanted by her as I was when she stepped out of our bedroom. To say she was worth waiting for tonight, hell, for my whole life, would still be an understatement. She's by far the most beautiful woman in the room, and I'm starting to think she would be the most gorgeous woman in any room.

The dress she has chosen is long, coming right down to her ankles. It's red, a color that looks absolutely delicious on her. The body of the dress is tight and fitted, but the skirt flows out slightly from the waist, so it billows when she walks. She's wearing high red heels that not only make her taller, but make her walk with more confidence and grace. Along with this, she's wearing a silver chain with a little rain drop shaped pendant on it and matching earrings.

She's not just stunning, she's a vision, and how I'm keeping my hands off her, I really don't know.

Except I'm not keeping my hands off her. Not really. The whole night I've either held her hand in mine, had my arm draped around her shoulders, or had my hand subtly on the small of her back to let everyone know she is mine. And at every opportunity, I've leaned in to steal a kiss.

I've introduced Ashley as my fiancée to my friends and family, to business associates and rivals, and it's not just because it's the polite thing to do, or because my mom would kill me if I introduced Ashley any other way at an event like this, where her friends and acquaintances are. But because I want to show her off. I want everyone to look at this vision of beauty and know she's mine.

I introduce Ashley to Joan, a friend of my mom's, a woman my parents have known for a long time.

Ashley smiles shyly and greets her, "It's a pleasure to meet you, Joan."

"Nonsense dear, the pleasure is all mine," Joan replies as she takes both of Ashley's hands in hers and air kisses her on each cheek.

I feel instantly jealous that she's touching Ashley instead of me touching her. I feel lost without some part of my body touching some part of hers. As soon as Joan releases Ashley's hands from hers, I take her hand again and kiss her cheek, feeling instantly better since I can feel Ashley's skin against mine again.

She smiles at me, although I can feel the tension in her body through her hand, the fear that she might say the wrong thing and risk the wrath of my mom, no doubt.

Joan makes an *aww* sound as she looks at the two of us. "Look at you two. So in love," she says with a dreamy sigh. "Are you nervous about the wedding, Ashley? I remember being where you are now, with my mother-in-law organizing this hugely extravagant wedding, and all I wanted was to marry John. I'd have been happy to do it in a quiet little ceremony, but that's not the way with these society types, is it?" Joan laughs and winks at me as she describes me as a society type.

Ashley relaxes a little, I feel her grip on my hand loosening. She has found a kindred spirit. "I'm not just nervous, I'm terrified," she confesses. "I would have liked an intimate little affair too. There's just so much that can go wrong with a big wedding isn't there? It's like there are hundreds of different moving parts that all need to come together perfectly and there are so many different ways I can mess up."

"Nothing will go wrong if Helen has anything to do with it, and I suspect she does." Joan pats her hand. "And you'll be fine. You want to know the best part of a big society wedding?"

Ashley nods.

Joan leans in conspiratorially. "Most of these people are secretly as out of their depths as we are. If you say or do something wrong, they'll assume they were the ones who had it wrong and that you're right. And even if it's some-thing major that they can't imagine away, they'll all just be so damned glad it wasn't them making a mistake that they won't mention it. And as the bride, the day is all about you. No one wants to be the one to upset a bride." She leans in a little further and winks at Ashley, talking in a practical whisper now, her eyes gleaming mischievously, "Seriously, if your dress falls down and you flash the guests during the ceremony, all of the clones will be so desperate to fit in, they'll probably all flash at you right back."

Ashley laughs and shakes her head. "I really hope it doesn't come to that."

"It won't, but it's always nice to have a backup plan, isn't it? Speeches getting a bit too long and boring? Flash and see who does it too. Used the wrong fork? Take a look around and see how many others have just followed suit. Seriously, after a few years of this, you'll learn to just laugh along with these types." Joan laughs.

Joan's husband, John, comes to join us. "There you are." He smiles at us. "Is she telling you stories about how everyone in this world is just one giant clone colony?"

I nod and smile.

John laughs and nudges Joan with his elbow. "You have to stop doing that, dear."

"Ah, let me have my fun. It's always nice to meet other people who feel the same way as I do."

"Come on," John cajoles. "Let's go and grab a drink before you convince Ashley to do something outrageous during her wedding, and Helen has a stroke or something,"

"Now that would be a scandal, wouldn't it?" Joan winks, but she allows John to lead her away from us.

"I'm sorry about her. She can be a little much," I say to Ashley.

"Don't be sorry. God Finn, she's the first person I've spoken to all night who has a bit of personality." Ashley giggles.

"I'll try not to take that personally," I joke.

"Obviously, I wasn't including you in that assessment. In fact, you've been right on form tonight. You've really been getting into playing the role of the attentive bridegroom to be."

"What if I told you it's no longer a role I'm playing, but the way I actually feel?" I ask, seriously. It's about time I fess up how I feel about her.

Ashley doesn't let me take the conversation down a more serious path, "I'd tell you that you'd had far too much champagne and call a cab for you."

"I'd better not say anything then."

"If you want to tell me things like that there's a whole tray of champagne over there with your name on it," she teases.

We head off in the direction of the waiter with a tray of champagne glasses. He sees us coming and steps to meet us, holding the tray out for us. We thank him and grab a glass each.

I point to an empty table and raise an eyebrow in question.

Ashley nods.

I lead her to the table and we sit down.

We've just sat down and start to sip on our champagne

when we're approached by a couple of clients of mine. They sit down and after I make the introductions, they start talking to Ashley about her charity work.

I can feel the champagne starting to have an effect on me. I'm actually enjoying this party, and it's the first one of these society parties I can ever say I've truly enjoyed. I know why. It has nothing to do with the party. It's all because I'm here with Ashley. I catch something my clients say, and it sounds like they might be interested in making a donation to Ashley's charity. It's her turn to shine without me hanging on to her like a dead weight. I put my hand on Ashley's arm to get her attention for a second.

"Excuse me," she tells the men and turns to me. "Is everything okay?" Her eyes beg me to let her get back into this conversation.

"Everything's fine. I'm just a little bit too hot, so I'm going to go out onto the balcony to grab some air," I whisper in her ear. "I won't be long."

"Ok." She nods. "I'll be here." She turns back to her conversation as I stand up and head for the large double doors leading outside. I look back at Ashley before I step outside. She's making a point she's passionate about; I can tell by the way her hands are moving. The two men she's talking to are hanging on her every word and I feel a pang of jealousy, which I push away. I don't need to be jealous. The most beautiful woman in the world is here with me.

I step out onto the balcony and move to stand against the railings. The cool air soon has me feeling refreshed and I'm just about ready to go back inside when my father joins me.

He stands beside me at the railings and lights a cigar. He smiles at me and then he looks out over the grounds of the house. "It's hot in there, isn't it?"

"Yes," I agree.

He falls silent for a moment and I think that is all he is going to say, but he turns to me. "You haven't told Ashley yet, have you?"

Shit. I didn't see this one coming. "No," I reply with a sigh.

"Are you in love with her?"

I haven't even told her I love her yet. I'm not about to tell my father first. "I'm just doing what needs to be done. Nothing more, nothing less," I inform levelly.

"But you and I both know it doesn't need to be done, don't we?"

"It's too late, Dad. Everything is in place for the wedding."

"I know you think you're rising to your grandpa's challenge or whatever nonsense you've cooked up in your head, but let me say this one thing and then I won't say another thing about this. There's nothing noble about marrying a girl you're not in love with."

"I didn't say it was noble, Dad. I said it had to be done," I point out. I turn to walk away and I freeze in my tracks.

Ashley is standing right behind us, and judging by the expression on her face, she's heard every word of our conversation.

My father seems to note the atmosphere has become both

charged and icy at the same time. He turns around and when he sees Ashley, he swallows hard. "Please excuse me," he mumbles before he throws his almost full cigar, still lit, into the ashtray and practically runs back into the party.

Great. He blows all of this shit up then runs away and leaves me to deal with the fallout.

"Ashley," I call, taking a step towards her.

"Don't come any closer, Finn," she commands in a low voice. "And don't even fucking think about touching me."

"You don't understand," I start.

"I understand perfectly well," she snaps, cutting me off before I can even begin to explain. "You weren't sure the money was enough of a reason for me to go through with this, so you played with my feelings, and made me believe there was something between us. You're a complete and utter bastard Finn Jagger, and I hate you. I absolutely hate you." She turns and runs.

I start to chase after her, but she's got a good head start. I really didn't see the running coming and she's already almost all the way across the room before I enter. I step around a waiter who tries to give me a glass of champagne, and by the time I get around him, she's gone.

I think maybe it's for the best. If I try to talk to her now, we'll only end up fighting. I decide to give her time to get home and cool down and then I'll go to her when I get home and we'll talk. We desperately need to talk.

I leave ten minutes after Ashley leaves the party. It's as long as I can bear to wait. I feel sick every time I think of the way she looked at me when she thought I was just playing with her. I don't want to lose her. I don't give a shit about the wedding. If we cancel it, we cancel it. But I need Ashley. I need her right by my side every day and every night. And I'm ready to tell her that.

I walk through the apartment and look in my bedroom, even though I know Ashley won't be in there. She'll have gone back to the guest bedroom to lick her wounds there. I move down the hallway to the guest bedroom and knock on the door.

Silence.

"Ashley, we need to talk."

Still silence.

"Ok, I'm coming in."

I wait a moment and then I take a deep breath and push the door open.

She's not there. The wardrobe doors are open and two of the drawers in the chest of drawers are open. And they're all empty.

Ashley has gone and the only thing remaining that tells me she was ever really here is the Lee Childs book she borrowed. It sits on the center of the duvet, mocking me as my heart breaks.

20

FINN

I've spent the whole weekend calling Ashley, leaving voicemails for her when she refuses to answer the calls. I've been sending her text messages and emails, all of which she has chosen to ignore. I have to see her, have to speak to her. Even if she still tells me to go to hell, at least I'll know I tried, and she'll know I wasn't using her.

At no time did I do that.

For all of Saturday and Sunday, I keep hoping she'll show up, and every time my phone rings, I answer it on the first ring letting myself hope it will be her, but she never shows up and none of the calls are from her.

I go into the office both days, which has become unusual for me over the last few weeks because now I finally have something to live for outside of the office.

I barely slept over the weekend, working until well after midnight and coming back to the office before six am. The apartment is just too quiet without her. Even at the office, a place that's always been my sanctuary, somewhere I can just forget all of my problems. To switch off, and just throw myself into my work, I'm suffering. I'm doing what needs to be done, but I feel like I'm just going through the motions, just doing things on autopilot.

No matter where I am or what I'm doing, all I can think about is Ashley.

I keep thinking of her arms and legs wrapped around me, her body glistening with sweat as I rock her world. I hear her moaning my name as she comes. Her face, like an angel above me. I can't believe I was blind enough to think she wasn't attractive when I first met her. She's easily the most gorgeous woman I've ever met.

When I'm not thinking about sex and Ashley's body, I'm thinking about her musical laughter, about the passion in her eyes when she talks about her charity and the way she throws herself into the path of danger at the drop of a hat if one of her kids needs her. The way she goes above and beyond for them.

Even in the few hours of restless sleep I have over the weekend, I don't have any reprieve from the mental torment of her. I dream of her constantly. In it, we are always having sex. Great sex. I tell her I love her and she says she loves me too. Then she laughs, a sound that echoes back to me a thousand times. Then I wake up and remember it was only a dream and the reality is... she hates me.

The very worst thing though, is how I can't get away from that hurt look she gave me before she ran from me at the party. It was a cross between contempt for me, and the look of someone who has been betrayed so badly they might never recover from the hurt. A look that said she hated me for letting her think I was different, a look so broken that it made me hate myself for putting it on her face.

I don't know what to do. I don't know if I've given her enough time to cool down. I'm scared if I approach her too soon when she's made it clear she doesn't want to talk to me, I'll only anger her further and she won't really hear what I'm saying.

But I'm scared that if I don't talk to her soon enough, she'll assume she was right and I don't give a flying fuck about her. And when I do try to talk to her, she'll think it's just an afterthought, a way to appease my own conscience, or worse to try and make sure the wedding still happens to save face.

The tension is making me crazy and I hate the out-of-control feeling. I need some advice. From someone who actually has a successful relationship. I mentally go through a few of my friends in my head, but none of them know my upcoming wedding is a sham, and by the time I've explained all of that, I'll just make Ashley look bad.

That really only leaves me with two options of who I can talk to about this. My mom or my dad. My mom won't be in the least bit impressed if she thinks I've hurt Ashley. Ashley has really grown on her over the last few weeks.

So my dad it is then. He's in a successful relationship, and to have negotiated his way through almost forty years of marriage with my mother, it's fair to say he knows how to handle a problem or two. He could probably write the book on how to talk his way out of tricky relationship situations with someone who is as stubborn as hell. Because that's both my mom and Ashley.

I pull my phone out of my pocket and call him. The phone is ringing now and it's too late to change my mind.

"Finn, what's up?" My dad answers.

"Ah not much, I'm just at work and thought I'd give you a call. What's up with you?"

"I'm okay," Dad says. "But I'm not the one making a seemingly pointless phone call in the middle of the work day. So stop pretending like everything's okay and tell me what's really going on."

My father is much more observant than I give him credit for. "You were right, Dad," I blurt out. "I do have feelings for Ashley. And she's so pissed off at me she won't even take my calls. I have to make her see that I love her and the only reason I denied it to you was because I hadn't told her yet."

"I knew it." There is great satisfaction in his voice.

"Yeah Dad, thanks for the *I told you so*. Now what do I do? How do I make her understand?"

"Does she feel the same way about you, Finn?" My dad asks.

"I hope so. I mean, I think she does. At least she did, but after what she overheard at the party, she now thinks I was just leading her on and acting like I felt something for her to make certain she went ahead with the wedding. So now, I'm not so sure."

"It's been three days since she overheard that conversation, Finn. She might be mad at you. She might even be wishing she'd never fallen for you, but she did. And feelings like those don't just go away in a couple of days, even when we so desperately want them to."

"God, I hope that's true."

"It's true," my father insists. "You want my advice? Go to her. She can ignore your calls, but it's a lot harder to ignore someone when they're right there in front of you. Talk to her, tell her how you feel, and admit that you're an idiot. She's known you for over three weeks now, Finn. It's fair to say she knows you're not exactly good at this stuff."

"Thanks for that, Dad," I answer dryly.

"It's true, isn't it? You're brilliant in the boardroom, but not so much when it comes to women."

"What if I do all of that and it still doesn't work?" I ask, ignoring his comment.

My father pauses for a second. "If that doesn't work, then you'll have to deal with the consequences of your actions and get over her. But is that really going to be any worse than it is now? At least if you know for sure it's over, you're not hanging in limbo and holding on to the hope of something that's never going to happen. But more importantly, what if it does work? What if she sees you're genuine and decides to forgive you? You'll have everything you ever wanted right there in front of you."

"Thanks, Dad," I say sincerely.

"Are you going to do it?" My dad asks.

"Yeah, Dad. I'm going to do it. I'm going over to her office right now." I laugh softly. "Holy shit! Yeah, I'm going to do it. I'm going to go and tell her I love her."

"Go get her, son," my dad encourages with a laugh.

I make my goodbyes and hang up. Grabbing my jacket, I rush out of my office. I'm really going to do this. Right now. "I have to go," I call out to my secretary. "Something important has come up, so clear my whole afternoon please."

"Got it," she announces, looking a little surprised to see me practically running out of my office.

I run to the elevator and wait impatiently for it. When it finally comes, I hop in and ride it to the ground floor. I hurry across the lobby and by the time I'm outside of the building, I'm actually sprinting towards the parking lot.

I get into my car and drive as fast as I can.

As I approach Ashley's office, adrenaline floods my system. I am excited and terrified in equal measure. All I have to do is convince Ashley that I love her and that I didn't want my father to know before she did, and then we can be together. But while it sounds simple, it's no small task. Ashley was hurt, really hurt, and I've seen how stubborn she can be. It's going to take a lot of work to get her to come around. But that's okay, because I'm willing to put the work in. I'll do whatever she wants, wait as long as it takes for her to see this is for real.

I pull up outside of Ashley's building and my jaw drops open. The building is all closed up, the shutters down. I get out of my car and look around, confirming I'm in the right place. I definitely am. I turn in a slow circle, looking around, as if the answer to what happened here is going to magically appear in front of me.

I mean I know Ashley was upset, but to not come in to work? That's not like her at all. And why didn't she get Andrea to open up the place if she couldn't face coming in?

Eventually, after standing here staring at the building for a few moments, wondering what's going on, I get back into my car. I think for a moment, then I pull my phone out and call Tyson and ask him to find Ashley's parents' address for me. I'm done waiting and I feel like if I don't do this today, now, I never will. If Ashley isn't at the office, then I'll just have to find out where she is and go there. I end the call and sit waiting impatiently for Tyson to get back to me with the address, tapping my fingers against the steering wheel the whole time.

She must be hurt really bad to not even have come to work. *God, what the fuck have I done? Nice going, Finn.*

I hear a light tapping sound on my window and I glance up.

A scruffy looking kid is standing beside my car.

The old me would have waved her away, shooed her from me like a nuisance stray cat, but the new me, the me Ashley teased out, doesn't try to get her to go away or ignore her. Instead, I open the window and look up at her. "What's up kid?" I ask.

"I'm sorry to bother you sir, but I wondered if you maybe had some spare change for a sandwich or something?" The girl asks.

I study her for a moment. She looks to be around fifteen and although she's a little dirty looking and her clothes have a few holes here and there, she doesn't look like she's high or drunk.

As I look at the girl, I hear Ashley's voice in my head as clear as if she was sitting right here beside me... imagine being fifteen and not having eaten for three days and not one of the adults who you encounter on a daily basis cares enough to help you.

"Sure," I say. I start rooting around in the glove compartment of my car looking for some change to give her. "Listen kid, do you have any idea what happened to the office here?" I point to Ashley's building.

"I wish I knew," the girl said. "The place was a charity that helped kids like me. The lady there would give us food and try to help us." The girl's eyes fill with tears. "She was contacting social services for me, trying to get me a place in a foster home. I guess that's over now."

"You wanted to go into the system?" I ask, a little surprised to hear it.

"No, sir. What I wanted was for my mom not to move in with her druggie boyfriend, but she chose him over me." She shrugs. "I guess a foster family has to be better than this shit, right?" She gestures around herself.

I stop rooting through the glove compartment and sit up to look at the kid. I make a snap decision in that moment. I'm going to help this kid. "Get in the car," I say.

The kid starts to back off and I realize how that must have sounded.

"Wait," I say quickly. "I'm sorry. I didn't mean it that way. Let me explain. The lady who ran the charity, Ashley, she's a friend of mine. Actually, she was more than a friend, but I screwed up and... never mind. Anyway, I know Ashley and she wouldn't have given up on you, so don't give up on her, okay? Get in the car and I'm going to take you and book you into a Travel Lodge where Ashley can contact you when she finds you somewhere. Would that be all right?"

I can see the dilemma in the girl's eyes. She so badly wants to trust me, but she's afraid. She's probably been let down so many times before that she's having a hard time thinking I can be anything but one of the bad guys.

"I'm trying to help you," I tell her gently. "What can I say to make this sound less creepy?"

The girl laughs softly and her eyes hold mine for a moment rather than flitting around looking for an escape route.

It breaks my heart a little to think she thinks there's a good chance I'm going to drive her off somewhere and do God knows what to her, and yet she hasn't fled because she's too hungry to run away from the possibility of a meal. Her laugh and the fact she's meeting my eye now gives me hope that maybe she can see I have good intentions.

"If you're serious, then there's a Travel Lodge just around this corner. We could walk there rather than me having to get into your car," she remarks quietly.

Her eyes are pleading with me to be serious about this, and her body is tensed, poised to run.

"Deal," I agree. "Why don't you back up a bit, so I can get out of the car without you feeling like I might grab you?"

She nods her head and backs up a little.

I roll the window back up and slowly get out of the car. I lock it and double check it's locked and then I turn to the girl. "Lead the way."

She starts walking and I walk with her, making sure to keep a safe distance between us.

She keeps giving me furtive glances as we walk and then finally she speaks up, "What's your deal?"

"What do you mean?" I ask.

"Not everyone is an opportunist dick that sees me as someone to be used, I'll admit that. But even the people who care would have given me a dollar or two and felt like they'd done their good deed for the day or whatever. But you're different. Why?"

This kid knows too much, has seen too much of how bad people can be. I shrug my shoulders. "I used to be that dick. Not the one who would have hurt you, but the one who would have told myself you ran away and brought this whole thing on yourself," I admit. "And on a good day, I would have done exactly what you said. Given you a couple of dollars and felt good about myself. On a bad day, I'd have shooed you away. But then I met Ashley and things changed. She made me see I'm part of the problem, and when she held up that mirror, I didn't like what I saw."

The girl seems to accept this and we fall back into silence for a moment before she speaks up again, "The last person before the charity lady who said they wanted to help me took me out to a parking lot and raped me. You know the worst part about that?" She looks over at me.

I shake my head, although I'm sure the worst part of that is the casual way she's speaking about it, like experience has taught her it's normal to be treated this way.

"Afterwards, he threw a twenty dollar bill at me and told he hadn't raped me, he'd used my services. I was so hungry I was grateful for the money."

"That's ..." I search for the right expression. "Hell kid, I don't even know what to say to that. That's... it's just not right."

"Yeah," she says with a shrug. "You have to find a way through it. If you want to not go completely crazy or turn to smack to get through the day, you have to find some other way to deal with shit like that. Mine is a twisted sense of humor I guess."

We reach the corner and turn it and I see the girl was right. A Travel Lodge sits on the corner of the next block. "What's your name?" I ask.

"Gemma," she answers. "What's yours?"

"Finn," I reply. "How long have you been on the streets?"

"Only about three months, but it already feels like too long."

"A day is too long."

"Yeah," she sadly replies.

"It's going to be okay, Gemma. Ashley... she's good at this stuff. She'll find a way to help you. I promise."

I know it's a promise Ashley might not be able to come through on, but there's something about this kid. She's seen too much, been through too much, but I get the feeling there's still hope for her. She's a little cynical, who wouldn't be at this point, but she doesn't seem like she's beaten. I admire her fighting spirit and I decide in that moment, if this foster thing doesn't work out, I'll make sure this kid is okay. If I have to pay for a little apartment for her while she finishes school and sorts herself out, then I will do it.

We reach the Travel Lodge.

Gemma hangs back a little watching me.

"What's wrong?" I ask.

"I guess I still hadn't let myself believe this was for real. I was waiting for you to laugh and walk away from me," she admits.

"That's not going to happen," I reassure her.

I want to say more, but I don't have the words to explain to someone like Gemma that not everyone who offers their help is a total dick. How can I convince her through words when every action she's seen up until this point argues against the idea? Actions speak louder than words and maybe by actually going through with this, she'll see that not everyone in the world is bad.

I pull the door to the Travel Lodge open and we go inside.

"Hi," I say to the woman at the reception desk. "I need to book a room. I don't want to know the number of the room, I just want to pay for it for the next month and add breakfast and dinner too."

The desk clerk stares at me like I've gone insane.

I have no way to explain this without humiliating Gemma.

Gemma, it seems, has no such qualms. "Don't look at him like that, he's trying to be nice. I'm homeless and he's getting me this room because... well because I think he's trying to impress a girl. And he doesn't want to know the room number, so I don't think he's a creep."

"Okay," the clerk says.

Gemma grins at me.

The desk clerk types into her screen for a moment and I hand her my card. I finish the transaction and nod to the couches at the back of the hotel lobby. "Get the key to your room. I'll be over here," I say and go sit down.

Gemma joins me a couple of minutes later with a key card in her hands. "Thank you," she says with tears shining in her eyes. She blinks quickly and recovers herself, grinning at me. "I hope Ashley is worth it."

"She is," I assert. "But this isn't just about impressing her. You know that, right?"

"Sure." Gemma shrugs.

I'm not convinced she does but I can live with her thinking I have an ulterior motive when it's only something as innocent as impressing Ashley. At least, I think Gemma has realized I don't have any intentions of hurting her in any way and that's enough for me. I want her to feel safe here. "I'm going to tell Ashley where you're staying so she can contact you, okay?"

Gemma nods.

"Do you need anything else? Clothes or anything?"

"No. You've done more than enough for me already. I have clothes in my backpack and now I have somewhere to wash them. And the room will have toiletries and everything. I can even wash my hair." She smiles at the thought of such a simple pleasure, one that I completely take for granted.

I nod and stand up. "It was nice to meet you, Gemma. And I really hope everything works out for you." I start to walk away.

"Two-seventy-nine," Gemma shouts.

I turn back. "Huh?"

"My room number. Just so you know I don't think you're like those others," She beams at me.

I smile back at her, touched by the gesture. Her trust is all she has to give and she's given it to me. "Good luck, Gemma."

Suddenly, she runs towards me and throws her arms around me.

I hug her back awkwardly for a moment.

She clings to me, holding me so tightly it almost hurts then she releases me and steps back. "And good luck to you too. Go get your girl." She turns and heads for the stairs.

I walk back to my car, satisfied that if nothing else, at least I've made a small difference to Gemma's life. I check my phone when I get back into my car and see I have three missed calls from Tyson. Helping Gemma is the first time in three days I haven't been thinking constantly of Ashley. The irony of that isn't lost on me.

I call Tyson back and he gives me an address. I thank him and plug it into my navigation system. It's in a nice area. At least, I won't be afraid to leave my car there.

I drive to the address and knock on the door. No matter what happens between us now, I have to speak to Ashley. Because it's not just about me anymore. It's about Gemma too.

21

ASHLEY

I know it's Finn at the door. I heard his voice before I slammed my bedroom door shut and went to lay on my bed. I can't believe he's got the nerve to show up here like this. I know my mom will get rid of him for me. She knows how much he's hurt me. Of course, she doesn't know the full story. If I had explained the marriage was never going to be real anyway, she would never have been able to understand why I'm so upset about it all. It's easier to just let her think Finn broke my heart the conventional way.

I hear footsteps on the stairs and then my mom knocks quietly on my bedroom door and pokes her head around.

"Ashley? It's…" she starts.

"I know who it is. And I don't want to see him. Please, just send him away."

"I told him all of that, honey, but he said he has some information for you about someone named Gemma?"

"What?" I say, sitting up from where I've been lying on my bed, a pillow hugged to my chest. "Who the hell is Gemma?"

"Some kid you were trying to place in the foster system or something?" My mom replies.

My eyes widen. Shit. How has he managed to find Gemma? And what does he know about her? "Is she hurt?" I ask.

"I don't know, love. Maybe you should go ask him yourself."

I sigh. He's played his hand well... I'll give him that. He knew this way I wouldn't be able to help myself from talking to him. "Fine. Send him up," resigning myself to the fact I'm going to have to see Finn, after all. I'm only going to talk to him about Gemma though. I have nothing else to say to him.

Mom nods and leaves my room.

I quickly jump up and look at myself in the mirror as I drag a comb through my hair. I don't care if I look a mess except for the fact I don't want Finn to think I'm like this, a total mess, because of him. Because I'm most definitely not.

I hear Finn coming up the stairs and I steel myself, although not enough to stop my stomach from turning over when I see how handsome he looks, but it's not enough to stop the pain inside me when I remember what he told his father.

"Your mom said it was okay to come up," Finn says.

"Well, you made damned sure I couldn't refuse, didn't you?" I snap. "Now what do you know about Gemma?"

"I went by your office and I ran into her. We got to talking and she told me you were trying to get her a place in a foster home. She's in the Travel Lodge around the corner from your office, so when you're ready to stop wallowing in self-pity and get your act together, that's where you can contact her. She'll be expecting your call."

"Wallowing in self-pity?" I repeat, my temper rising.

"Well, sure. Isn't that what you're doing here? Sitting here with the curtains drawn while crying over me, instead of helping the kids who have come to rely on you? Or do you have another word for it?"

I sit down hard on the bed, shaking my head, and glaring at Finn. "You've got some nerve, haven't you?" I snarl. "You think this is about you? My landlord called me on Saturday morning. He's got a buyer for our building and we're out. So no, I'm not wallowing in self-pity because of you. I'm on the verge of losing my charity altogether and I can't see any way out of that. So forgive me if I'm not doing the fucking cancan here."

"Shit Ashley, I'm sorry." He sits down beside me on the bed. "But it's not over. I can give you the two hundred and fifty thousand now and you can get some new premises, and—"

"Jesus Finn, how are you this fucking stupid?" I interrupt him. "Let me make it crystal clear for you. I don't want your money. I don't want anything from you anymore."

"It's good to know you haven't changed. You're still such a melodramatic brat," Finn mocks with a laugh.

His words shock me so much that I just stare at him, unable to form the words to tell him to just get the fuck out of here and not come back.

"You think that's unfair?" Finn is looking at me with a cool amusement, the way he used to look at me when we first met. "Well listen to yourself, Ashley. You're on the verge of losing your charity, and instead of thinking about the kids, you claim to care so much about, you're thinking about your damned pride."

"No, I'm not. I'm thinking that there's no amount of money in the world that will make me want to marry you now," I reply.

"Forget about the wedding for a moment."

"Oh, don't worry. It's forgotten," I shoot back sarcastically.

He shakes his head and goes on, "The money is a donation. And the monthly deal still stands. No matter what happens between us, you're getting that money. Believe it or not, Ashley, you have actually made me see the problems these kids face and I actually do want to help them. I don't know how best to do that, but you do, so it makes sense for me to donate the money to you and let you do what you do best."

"Right. And I'm supposed to believe there isn't a catch?"

"Oh, there's a catch," Finn adds quickly.

Here we go. I raise my eyebrows.

He smiles. "Help Gemma. Get her into the system and find her a place with a nice family. A family who will care about her and give her a chance."

"When did you grow a conscience?" I snap irritably.

"Well, according to Gemma, it was around the time I wanted to impress this girl," he teases with a lopsided smile.

The way he looks just now makes my heart melt. But if he thinks being cute is going to work on me, he's very much mistaken. My heart might respond to him, and my body certainly does, but for once, I'm doing things Finn's way and making the decisions with my head instead of my emotions. "It didn't work. You didn't impress me in the slightest" I lie. I am kind of impressed he's willing to help someone like Gemma. But it's too little too late as far as I'm concerned. "Thank you for helping Gemma. Now if you don't mind, I have things to do."

He makes no move to leave. He doesn't even get up off the bed. He just nods his head slowly, like he's thinking about something. "Yeah, I see that. I mean your pillow isn't going to cry into itself, is it?"

"Why are you taking so much pleasure in my misery?" I demand.

"I'm not," he answers quietly. "But I know you. And I know you'll rise to the challenge if one is put in front of you."

"Whatever," I say, although I have to admit he's nailed it. I'm already planning things in my head. "You went to the office looking for me before you even met Gemma, so why don't you tell me why you're really here?"

Maybe if I pretend to hear him out and then tell him to leave, he'll actually go. It's the only reason I asked him why he's here. It's not like I care what he has to say anymore. Not even a little bit.

This is my moment. My chance to tell Ashley everything. But the way she's looking at me with such disdain, the way she's made it clear she's only entertaining talking to me because I had news on Gemma, tells me it's a waste of time.

It's too late for Ashley and me and to be honest, I would rather her remember me as the guy who helped a homeless kid, instead of the guy who stood begging for her approval. I stand up. "I came here to tell you I'm sorry about what happened at the party, and to try to explain it all to you. But it's clear you don't want to hear it, and so I'm just going to go. You can call me anytime if you need anything for the charity."

I move my hand towards my pocket to pull out the check I've already written.

"You know for a long time I thought you were arrogant and

only into yourself," she explains. "Sometimes, I still do. But I never thought you were a coward until now."

"Excuse me?"

"You're here. I'm here. You have your chance to finally tell me the truth, but you're too much of a coward to take it," Ashley snaps back. She looks at me, staring straight into my eyes. A challenge.

"You want the truth? Fine. Here it is. The truth is, I do care about you, Ashley."

"No, you only care about getting your hands on your grandpa's company," she counters. "You said as much to your father."

"That's not true," I counter.

"Oh, really?" Ashley sneers.

"Yes, really." I sit back down on the bed. "Aren't you the least bit curious about why my father suddenly thought I had feelings for you?"

Ashley shrugs.

"He thought it, because he saw it, Ashley. And he knew something you don't. He knew that my grandpa had a change of heart. There's another will. One dated later than the original one, where my grandpa came to his senses and removed the marriage stipulation. So I can marry you, or not marry you, and either way, I get the company. I found out the night I went to my parent's house for dinner."

"And it didn't occur to you to tell me that?" Ashley gasps.

"I was going to tell you that night, but you were stressed out because you'd lost your assistant. I decided to wait until the next day. But then we had that talk, and I thought if I told you then, you would think I was trying to put you off or something. I don't know what I really thought. I was just scared if you found out we didn't have to go through the marriage you wouldn't want to. That... I would lose you." I explain.

"So you hid it from me?" Ashley sighed.

"Yes. But I did plan on telling you. I just never found the right moment. But that's not the point. The point is, I lied to my father. I lied to him because I hadn't told you I loved you, and I figured you should hear that before my father did. Because that's the truth that matters. Ashley Winters, I love you. With every fiber of my being. And I can't imagine my life without you in it."

I don't know what reaction I'm expecting, but it sure as hell isn't the one I get.

Ashley jumps to her feet, her face contorted with rage. She points to the door. "Get the hell out of here Finn and don't fucking come back," she yells.

"What? No," I argue, getting to my feet, but not leaving. "I mean it, Ashley. I swear I'm telling you the truth. I love you."

"And so you thought it was okay to essentially con me into marrying you? You say you were going to tell me about the new will, but when Finn? After we were married?"

"No. Maybe. I don't know. I'm sorry okay. I didn't think of it like that. I just—"

"Of course, you didn't think of it like that. You didn't fucking think at all. You just saw something you wanted and decided you were going to take it, didn't you?"

She's still yelling, but I've kind of switched off from it. This was a mistake. And coming here has only made it worse. Surely, for her to be this angry, that has to mean she feels something for me? "Ashley!" I shout loud enough to be heard over her tirade.

She stops and glares at me.

I reach into my inner pocket to pull out the check and hand it to her. "I will be keeping my word to you about the donation whether you like it or not. The only condition is that you help Gemma."

She nods.

That much at least I know she'll do.

"And as for the wedding, I'm not going to cancel it."

"What?" She demands.

"I said I'm not cancelling the wedding. Because I hope you'll think about this and realize that I fucked up massively, but that I'm sorry. I hope you'll give us a chance. So here's the deal. Come to the wedding, marry me, but only if there's a little part of you that feels the same way about me, a little part of you that's willing to give us a shot."

"I won't be there, Finn," Ashley snaps.

I head for the bedroom door then turn back to look at her. "Just think about it okay?"

I leave before she can answer. I know the next five days are going to be the longest five days of my life.

23

FINN

I feel like every eye in the room is on me as I stand at the altar on the raised platform at the front of the grand ballroom of Melbourne Hall. A lot of the people filing in probably are looking at me.

After all, it is my wedding they're here for after all. But I don't feel as though they're looking at me out of interest, or because it's expected of them to look interested or whatever. I feel as though they're all looking at me and pointing the finger, blaming me for what's about to come. That would be fair I guess. It is my fault after all.

In a couple of hours, they could all be sneering at me, since Ashley most likely isn't going to show up to the wedding at all. It could turn out to be one big joke that everyone is in on except for me. Ashley made it abundantly clear she wasn't going to show up today, but I refused to cancel it.

She's going to have to stand me up if she doesn't want to get married today.

Over the last few days, I've gone back and forth about whether or not I think she will show up today. One moment, I'm sure she's going to show up. The next minute, I'm equally as sure she won't. It's been absolute hell, but I can't complain. I mean I brought the whole thing on myself. God, why did I have to be so fucking stupid?

The thing is, I wasn't consciously trying to hide anything from Ashley or force her hand. It wasn't until Ashley's angry reaction to the truth about how I felt about her and the revised will, was I able to see for myself how fucked up it was not to have told her the truth sooner.

In my mind at the time, I suppose I thought it was romantic, but looking at it through Ashley's eyes, I can see why she felt angry. I can see why she thought I was trying to force her to marry me whether she wanted to or not.

I suppose in some ways I was, but not in a creepy *'you'll marry me whether you like it or not'* sort of a way. More, in my mind at least a, *'I love you and I just want you to see that maybe you could feel the same about me once you really get to know me'* sort of a way.

"Are you okay man?" My best man Toby asks, putting his hand on my shoulder. He is peering at me like he doesn't quite know what to make of me and his face is creased with concern.

"Yeah, sure. Why wouldn't I be?"

"I don't know. But you look really white, like you're going to flake out on me or something," he replies.

"I'm just nervous," I reassure, forcing a smile.

Just nervous. There's an understatement. I know you're meant to be a little nervous on your wedding day, but it's meant to be about saying the vows wrong, or the flowers not showing up, and maybe a tiny bit of *will she come or won't she come* type of nerves. Maybe even a few nerves about how well you'll be able to perform in bed after a long day filled with too much booze and too much food.

But I'm pretty sure it's not meant to be because the odds of the bride turning up are slim to none. Realistically, I'm putting the odds at eighty - twenty, that's an eighty percent chance she won't show up. But despite all of this, there's still a tiny bit of hope inside of me. I've defied the odds before and maybe, just maybe, I can do it again.

I look at my watch for what feels like the one hundredth time since I got up here. There's another six or seven minutes to wait before Ashley is even due and I know without a doubt they're going to be the longest minutes of my life. To distract myself, I look around the hall.

It's a big hall with huge crystal chandeliers hanging from the ceiling, the lights are dimmed enough to give the place a dreamy, romantic atmosphere. And the whole place is covered in camellias.

I scan the crowd to see a lot of familiar faces, before I spot Ashley's family in their seats, minus her dad who is likely pacing around somewhere himself. I'm not sure if seeing them here is a good thing or a bad thing. It's good that they're here at all, surely Ashley would have told them if she wasn't going to be here? But they look on edge, looking at their watches and shuffling uncomfortably in their seats, as though they too think there's a fair chance Ashley isn't about to walk down the aisle.

I hear movement behind me and I turn around.

Our minister, who insists we don't need all of the formality and we should just call him Kevin, has arrived from behind his little side door. "Finn," he smiles warmly, taking my hand in his and pumping it enthusiastically. "You look nervous."

"I am," I admit. I don't elaborate. A wedding is one of the few occasions where no one expects you to elaborate on why you're nervous.

"You think this is bad," Toby jokes, "wait until it hits him what he's about to do and he makes a run for it."

I frown at him.

"Relax man. It's just a joke," he hisses under his breath and starts to laugh.

Kevin doesn't seem to know quite what to say to this. He smiles awkwardly at Toby and then keeps shooting me furtive little glances, like he thinks I might be a flight risk or something. If only he knew, it isn't me he should be worrying about.

I look back out into the hall. Pretty much everyone is seated now. Every seat is filled except the one waiting for Ashley's dad after he walks her down the aisle, and it is a lot of people to witness my shame, or rather my mom's shame, and my heartbreak.

I check my watch again, as the groomsmen begin to file out

of the back of the room as arranged. They'll wait there for their bridesmaids and walk down the aisle with them. There's less than a minute to go and from the quick flash of the hallway I get when the groomsmen are filing out, there isn't a bridesmaid in sight.

And it's not like they have any reason to be late. Except the obvious one, they know something I don't. There won't be any traffic jams or flat tires or any of that kind of stuff. Everyone in the wedding party, and to my knowledge the majority of the guests, have rooms here to stay overnight after the reception party, so they all have somewhere on the site to get ready too.

"Where are they?" I ask Toby.

"Relax Finn. It's almost like a rule these things start a couple of minutes late," he whispers back. "She'll be here, don't worry." His expression seems a little bit more worried than his casual tone, though. He's frowning and checking his watch too.

Even the guests are starting to get restless, shuffling in their seats. The quiet hub-bub of whispered conversation has gone up a notch as people start to speculate about the time.

At this point, the music starts to play. It's a moving classical piece with gentle notes that carry well across the large space. It seems to calm the guests, making them settle back down and start to smile.

The door opens and Ashley's maid of honor, Sophie, steps in. She's wearing a long dress in midnight blue satin, the color an exact match for the voile on the chairs. Sophie is smiling as she walks slowly down the aisle. This cannot be anything but a good sign?

Toby moves to meet Sophie as she reaches the end of the aisle, offering her his arm as she arrives at the platform. He helps her up onto it.

I turn my focus back to the door.

Already the other bridesmaids and the groomsmen are walking down the aisle in their pairs.

They reach the platform and step up, the groomsmen coming to stand behind me. Toby arranges himself at the front of their little line, directly behind me. The bridesmaids line up behind the maid of honor.

The classical music slowly fades out, replaced by the opening notes of the wedding march. The mood in the whole hall changes to one of excited expectation when the music starts.

I watch the door, my heart racing. My mouth is dry and my palms are sweaty.

It's been too long. Too long since the rest of the wedding party came in.

I notice Toby exchanging what he thinks are subtle looks with the maid of honor.

She looks horrified, and she keeps mouthing *I don't know.*

Does this mean she doesn't know why Ashley has fled, or she doesn't know why she's running a minute or two late?

It's too late for me to have any hope of Ashley being here.

The maid of honor clearly doesn't know why Ashley isn't here. For all I've tried to steel myself for this inevitable moment, deep down, I realize now, I thought she would come.

I really did.

I realize something else as well. I have absolutely no idea what to do next. Do I make an announcement that Ashley isn't coming, or do I slip out of the side door and let Toby and the minister handle the guests?

I've never really thought much about marriage except in the abstract, until I met Ashley. So needless to say, the etiquette of being stood up at the altar has definitely passed me by.

I glance at the minister, hoping to take my cue from him.

He's smiling serenely, the same expression he has worn since the maid of honor appeared, but now, it looks forced.

It doesn't help me in the slightest. I don't think anyone can help me at this point. I should just leave. Somehow, I can't make my feet move though and I keep my eyes on the minister's face, as though by looking at him, I can somehow force this all to be okay. He definitely is the one who will know what to do next I tell myself.

As I watch him, trying to get his attention without it being obvious to the guests that's what I'm doing, his face changes. His smile looks genuine again now, and his shoulders have relaxed. A pleased sigh comes from the guests.

Now, I dare to let myself think she's here.

I don't turn around to look though in case I am wrong and

the tiny spark of hope inside of me dies for good. Then I hear a gasp rise up from the crowd and I know it can only mean one thing. I slowly turn around.

My heart almost stops in my chest when I see Ashley and her father moving slowly down the aisle towards me. Even through the long veil she's wearing, I can see Ashley is smiling, and her cheeks are flushed pink. She's carrying a large bouquet filled with white lilies and midnight blue roses.

Her dress is pure white, the bodice tight and strapless, adorned with silver thread that shines beneath the light from the chandeliers. The skirt part of the dress is fuller, billowing out around her legs in swirls of voile and satin, shot through with the same silver thread. It makes her look ethereal. They have done something with her hair too, made it look as if it is very long while put into a bun at the back of her head and decorated with flowers.

She is a vision and I know without a doubt that she is by far the most beautiful thing I have ever seen or will ever see again. My heart is hammering in my chest, a remnant of my total panic from earlier, but I can swallow again, which is something. I still feel nervous, but the urge to throw up or flake out has passed. Now I feel like this is normal wedding nerves, and all of those things I had blocked out worrying about when I was solely focused on whether or not Ashley would even show up, come rushing back in.

What if I make a mistake with the ring? Oh God, what if the ring is missing?

I tell myself none of it matters. All that matters is that I'm marrying the woman of my dreams, and it is the one thing

I'm certain isn't a mistake. It never could be. I still can't resist glancing at Toby and mouthing, *"You have the ring?"*

He nods and pats his jacket on the spot where the inner pocket is.

I turn my gaze directly back to watch Ashley. I know it's a cliché, but I really do only have eyes for her.

Ashley and her father reach the edge of the platform. She turns to face him for a moment.

He takes her hands in his and gently squeezes them.

Ashley and her father turn back to the platform.

Toby nudges me forward.

I remember what I'm supposed to be doing and I step forward.

Ashley's father places her hand in mine, and nothing has ever felt so right. My whole body tingles from her touch as I watch her step onto the platform beside me.

She turns to face me.

I reach up and take her veil in my hands. My hands are shaking, but I ignore the nerves and slowly lift the veil and push it back. She's wearing a silver and diamond tiara in her hair and I can see it now since the veil is pulled back, but I see it for only a second before my eyes lock on hers.

Her cheeks are flushed and glowing, but she looks nervous too.

I want to reach out and hold her, to wrap her in my arms and never let her go, but I know I can't do that yet. I settle for leaning in close to her and whispering in her ear, "You look beautiful."

She's smiling when I stand back, tears shining in her perfectly made up eyes. She mouths a *thank you* at me and then I take her hand in mine and we turn to face the minister.

"Welcome ladies and gentleman, and thank you for coming together today to stand witness as Finn and Ashley celebrate their love for each other and become one. Marriage is not something to be entered into lightly. It's a life-long commitment to love each other. And it is not really about today. Although today marks the first day of their journey together, marriage is about so much more than simply a wedding. It is about being there for each other through the good times and the bad times. It is about supporting each other, and becoming a team that will always stand together, no matter what."

As he says the words, I risk a glance at Ashley. I expect her to look angry somehow, but she doesn't.

She looks happy. She must feel my eyes on her because she turns her head to face me, and smiles at me.

Kevin is reading a poem now, one no doubt chosen from an approved list of my mother's recommendations. I barely hear the words, focusing instead on Ashley, and for a minute, I am filled with regret. Not regret that I am marrying Ashley, but regret that I'm not giving her the wedding of her dreams. I'm giving her the wedding of my mom's dreams.

I realize Kevin's words at the start of the ceremony were true, perhaps truer for us than any other couple. Marriage isn't about the wedding. It's about being together in spite of the odds. It's about having each other's backs through everything that comes up over a lifetime together. It's about being by each other's sides through thick and thin.

Kevin finishes the poem and now he's addressing us.

I force my eyes from Ashley and focus on his words. I'm bound to get something wrong if I'm not even listening to him.

"Marriage is a contract between two people, make no mistake about that," Kevin continues.

Ashley glances at me and gives me a smug grin.

"But it's not a contract written solely in black and white. It's a contract between two hearts. Two hearts that promise to love each other for all eternity," he goes on.

Now, it's my turn to flash Ashley a smug grin.

Maybe we're both right. Maybe marriage is a contract, but maybe it's also about love and celebrating our relationship.

"And now the vows," Kevin says. "Finn, repeat after me. I, Finn, take you, Ashley, to be my lawfully wedded wife. To have and to hold, in sickness and in health, until death parts us."

I repeat his words without stumbling, looking into Ashley's eyes as I say the words, needing her to know that although I didn't write the words, my mom thought writing our own vows would be tacky, especially given the situation when we were first planning all of this, I mean them with everything I am and everything I have.

"And now Ashley, repeat after me. I, Ashley, take you, Finn, to be my lawfully wedded husband. To have and to hold, in sickness and in health, until death parts us," Kevin repeats.

Ashley looks at me and smiles, her unshed tears catching the light from above, making her eyes even more luminous than usual. "I, Ashley, take you, Finn, to be my lawfully—"

She stops abruptly as the door at the end of the aisle slams open.

Everyone turns to see what's going on and every eye in the place lands on Andrew Garfield.

My heart sinks into the bottom of my stomach.

Andrew is storming down the aisle towards us, a brown envelope in his hand as everyone watches him, whispering and looking at each other in horror.

Ashley looks at me questioningly.

"My grandpa's lawyer," I whisper.

"Excuse me sir, you can't just come in here like this," Kevin says, trying and failing to remain serene.

"I apologize for the dramatic entrance, but I'm a lawyer and something of the utmost legal importance has just been brought to my attention," Andrew announces.

I glance at my mom.

She's stone white and looks ready to pass out, kill someone, or both.

"Finn, listen..." Andrew gets closer to me, talking in hushed tones.

I know everyone in the room is straining to hear what's being said.

"Your grandfather made a new will. It's just been brought to my attention and the marriage clause is gone. You don't have to marry Ashley to inherit your grandfather's shares in the company." He at least has the decency to shoot Ashley an apologetic look as he finishes up his revelation.

"Yes, I do," I declare.

"No..." Andrew starts.

I reach out and take the envelope. "Yes, I do, because I'm in love with her." I pull the new will from the envelope. "You don't have a copy of this right?" I ask.

"No," he replies looking so confused, I almost pity him. He doesn't know he's making a scene at our wedding. He thinks he's saving us from making a massive mistake.

I hold the will in both hands and look at Ashley who nods. I rip it in half and in half again. I keep ripping it until it's in tiny pieces and then I drop the torn pieces into his palm. "Thank you, Andrew. That will be all. Drinks and hors d'oeuvres will be served on the front lawn in a little over thirty minutes if you'd like to stay."

He just stands there, his mouth open, looking from me to Ashley to the torn up will and back at me again.

"Mr. Garfield," my mom calls from behind Andrew.

"Ah, Helen. I was just explaining to Finn that—"

"Your services are no longer required Mr. Garfield," she snaps.

Andrew finally starts to move away from us, still looking confused.

My mom turns to face the guests who are all whispering amongst themselves. "It would appear that my father-in-law's lawyer has some serious boundary issues," she says in a measured voice. "But please don't let him ruin this day for my son and my new daughter." She turns back to me as the guests settle down and she smiles.

I smile back at her. I know this is going to be talked about in the society for years to come. Not so much Andrew's appearance, as legal matters aren't talked about, but his outburst, because no matter how controlled it was, that's what it will be seen as. And in that moment, my mom didn't care about her society friends and what they might think – she only cared about Ashley and me.

My mom heads back to her seat, but not before Ashley clasps her hand quickly and squeezes it. My mom is beaming when she sits back down.

Kevin seems at a loss for how to get things back on track.

Ashley smiles at me, and then in a voice that is soft yet carries across the whole hall, she says her vows, starting over again from the beginning, "I, Ashley, take you, Finn, to be my lawfully wedded husband. To have and to hold, in sickness and in health, until death parts us."

I'm impressed at how composed she is, but mostly, I'm

impressed she still remembers exactly what she's supposed to say.

This gets things moving again and Kevin quickly recovers himself, asking for the rings. We exchange rings and Kevin reads another poem.

This time, I do listen to the reading and it's a captivating poem about love and living a life together with someone, two hearts living as one.

When he's finished, I have to blink quickly to remove the haze of warm tears settling in my eyes. I hope the words are enough to remind everyone why we're here today and to have them forget about Andrew's interruption. I know it'll be talked about; I just hope it's not today. Because today... should be only about love.

"I now have the honor of pronouncing you two husband and wife," Kevin exclaims with a big smile. "Finn, you may kiss the bride."

I cup Ashley's face in my hands and kiss her full on the mouth. My whole body lights up as we kiss, Ashley's arms slips around my neck. I move my hands away from her face to put my arms around her waist and dip her slightly.

As I dip her, the guests start to clap and cheer... then I remember where I am. For a moment there, it felt like it was just the two of us, like we were the only two people in the world, let alone in this room. I quickly pull Ashley back upright when I remember myself and move my lips back from hers.

She smiles as we look into each other's eyes. I feel like I am looking into my future. And it's going to be a bright future indeed.

WE SIGN the marriage license with Toby and Sophie acting as our witnesses, and now, we walk down the aisle together as a married couple. Mr. and Mrs. Jagger. I love how that sounds.

As we leave the hall, I get a quick glimpse of the grounds set up for our reception. Wooden tables and chairs are scattered across the perfectly manicured lawn and flowers are everywhere. Each table has a stunning floral centerpiece. A large stage has been erected alongside the hall for the band and later on, for the DJ. Wait staff dressed all in black are milling around with silver trays waiting for their roles to start.

We are approached almost instantly by a waiter who smiles at us, congratulates us and then hands us each a glass of champagne. I gulp mine down gratefully and I bite my tongue to keep from laughing when I see Ashley doing the same thing beside me.

I have barely finished it when the glass is whipped out of my hand as Ashley and I are led away from the reception area followed by the wedding party and our parents for the photographs. We're taken to a beautiful lake on the grounds of Melbourne Hall. Then we spend the next hour standing in various combinations and poses. I'm sure the photographer is world famous, although I have no idea who he is, and he certainly seems to know what he's doing. He won't take a shot until the lighting and everything is perfect. I think this will start to irritate Ashley, but when I look at her, she's beaming so wide it must be hurting her cheeks.

For perhaps the first time since I arrived at the hall this morning, I relax a little bit. Ashley is here. She's my wife. *My actual wife.* She looks so happy, today wasn't just about her not wanting to make a scene, but about us being together. We have a lot to discuss, but the fact she came at all tells me she sees a future for us. She wouldn't have come here and married me if she didn't. I see that now.

The photographs are finally all taken and we move to the reception area which is now filled with our guests. The band starts playing as we appear and a cheer goes up from the guests. I smile at Ashley and she smiles back at me. I lead her to the head table and we sit down to a wonderful three course meal. We talk through the meal, of course we do, but it's light chatter and I'm starting to feel the weight of the real talk we need to have pressing down on me. Once the meal is over and the speeches are all done, I take Ashley by the hand and lead her away from the crowd. She follows me without question, and I think she knows as well as I do, this conversation can't wait any longer.

I lead her back to the lake where we had our photos taken. I remove my jacket and spread it on the ground for Ashley.

She smiles at me and sits down on it, protecting her dress from any tell-tale grass stains. I sit down beside her and for a moment, we're quietly content in each other's company, looking out over the lake, each filled with our own private thoughts.

Now I have her here and I don't know where to start, but it's clear to me that she's not going to be the one to start the conversation. So eventually, I blurt out the one thing I've wanted to say to her all day, "you came."

"It looks that way." She smiles.

"I didn't really think you would come," I admit.

She smiles again. "Honestly Finn, I didn't really think I would myself," she mutters in a voice so quiet it's almost a whisper.

I swallow hard. Is it all just a dream? Did she do it just to save face and now, she's going to tell me it's over between us anyway? Surely, she wouldn't be so cruel. She takes my hand in hers and squeezes it gently and I think maybe I'm right and it's not that at all. She turns her head to look at me and I shuffle slightly, so I'm facing her.

"I was so angry with you for not telling me the truth about the will. I told myself I hated you and I never wanted to see you again. The thing is though, it wasn't true. I don't hate you. I love you, just in case you haven't guessed that part. I knew I would regret it for the rest of my life if I didn't take a chance on us, because both of us kind of fuck everything up pretty regularly. But we're good together and to be honest, I can't imagine my life without you in it."

"We do have a habit of fucking things up, don't we?" I chuckle.

"Yes," Ashley deadpans, while looking me square in the eye. "And it has to stop. We can't live the rest of our lives in uncertainty, or running through a constant series of misunderstandings and fights. Although... the makeup sex is kind of worth it."

We laugh at this as we both think of the amazing angry sex we've shared.

"Seriously though, Finn, we need to learn to talk to each other. About the big stuff as well as the small stuff," she continues. "Even if it seems scary or we know it will make the other angry. We just have to suck it up and do it."

"I know," I agree. "And I know how close I came to losing you and I won't let that happen again, Ashley. I swear from now on, I won't keep anything from you ever again." I think of the envelope in my pocket, the one I haven't told her about yet, and I look away from her for a moment. Here I am promising not to keep anything from her again, and already I'm lying to her. I think she might forgive me for this one, when she finds out what's in the envelope.

"Let's just start over from now," Ashley beams. "No dwelling on the past."

"That works for me." I grin at her. "So helping Gemma really did impress you."

She laughs softly.

"It did. But it didn't make me want to marry you. I already wanted that."

"So you don't think marriage is just a contract anymore?" I ask with a raised eyebrow.

"I kind of liked how Kevin put it. A contract between two hearts." She nods.

"Me too," I agree.

"Speaking of Gemma, you'll be pleased to know I've found her a family. She'll be moving in with them sometimes next week. She's so excited Finn and I've met the family and they seem really nice. They're an older couple with plenty of experience of fostering kids and they're really excited to have her move in too. I think they'll get a pleasant surprise when she does move in. They're used to dealing with problem kids, but Gemma was never the problem in her home."

"That's amazing news," I whisper as I lean in and kiss Ashley. I feel fire flood through my body. What started out as a tender kiss is fast becoming something more and I feel my cock hardening as Ashley runs her hands over my body. I pull back from the kiss and smile at her, shaking my head. "We have to stop," I breathe.

"Why?" she questions with a teasing smile.

I glance down at my crotch where it's clear my cock is ready for her. "We're kind of in a public place," I caution.

"Ooh... you're a prude!" Ashley laughs.

"Not at all." I smirk. "But the thought of getting grass stains all over your dress and then going back to the party doesn't really feel like a good plan."

Ashley smiles at me, her head down, then she peeks up at me through her long eyelashes. She bites her bottom lip for a moment. "Well, we could always slip away to my room for a bit," she suggests.

I get to my feet and lower my hand to help her up. "I thought you'd never ask!" I laugh.

We move towards the building, slip in a back door so none of our guests will see us sneaking away. We get into the elevator, giggling. We barely manage to keep our hands off each other the whole way up, so by the time we reach Ashley's room and she pulls a key card from the bodice of her dress, I am almost delirious with lust for her.

I pull her into my arms before the door to the room has even closed behind us, my lips seeking hers out and finding them smooth, moist and eager for mine. I kiss her hard, passionately, hoping my kiss shows her that I know how close I came to losing her and that I am so happy to have her back.

She pulls my shirt out of my slacks and begins to open my fly. She reaches in as she pushes the slacks and my boxers down slightly. She grabs my cock and begins to move her hand up and down it.

I feel fire flooding through my body and I begin to walk Ashley towards the bed. We reach it, but she hangs back and I move my mouth from hers. "Is something wrong?" I ask. Her hand on my cock doesn't feel like anything's wrong, but I can't understand why she doesn't want to get on the bed.

"I don't want to wreck my dress," Ashley warns quietly, looking self-conscious, her cheeks turning red.

I can't help but laugh, after the way she protested against having a designer wedding dress at all, she's now worried she might wreck it, but I guess I understand. I move around her so I'm behind her and slowly unzip the dress. She makes a gasping sound as I run my fingers over her bare shoulders after unzipping the dress.

I lower it to the floor and she steps out of it. I take it and lay it carefully over the chair in the corner of her room. "Is that better?" I turn back to her and she takes my breath away with her in lacy white panties and no bra.

In answer to my question, she slips her panties down, steps out of them, closes the gap between us, and throws herself into my arms, her lips finding mine again.

This time, there's no resistance when I move her towards the bed. I push her back onto the mattress and take a moment to get out of my own clothes, not being in the least bit careful about where they end up. I just want to be inside of Ashley.

I push her thighs open and lean towards her pussy, needing to taste her first.

"Finn, we have guests waiting. I think we just need to be quick," she insists.

I run my tongue over her labia and find her clit. I work it beneath my tongue until Ashley is panting and grasping the duvet in her balled fists. I pause for a moment, looking up at her. "Are you sure you want this to be quick?" I grin.

"Screw the guests," she moans.

I'm grinning when I go back to work on her clit. I work her until she comes hard, liquid soaking her thighs. She's still gasping for breath when I crawl up her body and kiss her lips. Her hands grasp at me, her arms pulling me down on top of her.

I slip inside of her, her tight little pussy sucking me in and dousing me in her juices. God I've missed this. I've missed her.

I begin to move, slowly at first, wanting to make this last, but I'm still fired up from Ashley's hand job earlier and I know I won't be able to last as long as I want to. I begin to move faster, spurred on by the fire in my belly and Ashley's moans in my ear.

When she comes again, her pussy is clenching around my cock and it sends me over the edge, and we come together, both of us moaning each other's name. The pleasure spreads through my body, making me feel warm all over. I roll off Ashley and lay beside her for a moment while I catch my breath. I sit up once I feel like I can breathe normally again. "We really should get back to the reception," I sigh.

"I know," Ashley agrees, sitting up beside me. She kisses my shoulder. "We're like animals, can't control ourselves for even a second."

"Yeah and I wouldn't change it for the world."

"Same," Ashley agrees.

I get dressed again, and then I help Ashley back into her dress. After I close the zipper, I pull her back against me and wrap my arms around her waist. I press my lips against her neck and then I whisper into her ear, "I love you so much Ashley. You really are the best thing ever to happen to me."

She puts her hands on my arms. "I love you too, Finn." There's a smile in her voice when she goes on, "Now enough of this or I'm going to end up crying and wrecking my make-up." She turns to face me.

I kiss her full on the lips again.

She scurries away from me to the dresser and peers into the mirror for a second. She tidies up her hair with her hands and reapplies her lipstick then she turns back to me. "There. No one will ever know where we've been now."

I refrain from pointing out the post orgasmic glow all over her face and chest. Instead, I take her hand and lead her back out of the room. We go back down in the elevator, laughing about what we've just done, then we cross the lobby and step outside. The party is in full swing now with drinks flowing and people up dancing.

"Where have you been?" My mom calls as she spots us and comes storming over to us. "The band has been calling for you two to do your first dance."

"Sorry, Mom. We... umm... got caught up."

"Doing what?" She demands as she looks at Ashley and sees the flush of her cheeks then she reddens slightly. "Oh... well, never mind. You're both here now. I'll let the band know you're ready for your first dance." She flits back away leaving Ashley and me laughing.

"Well *that* was embarrassing," Ashley whispers.

"But on the plus side, it got rid of her," I point out.

"I should have told her we were having sex ages ago and I might have gotten out of all of those planning sessions." Ashley laughs.

"About that," I say. "I'm sorry this wasn't the wedding you would have chosen."

"No, Finn. It's absolutely perfect." She smiles dreamily. "Granted, it's not necessarily what I would have chosen, but seeing it all now, your mom actually has damned good taste."

"Well, she made me, didn't she?"

Ashley elbows me in the ribs. "Ok, enough of that Mr. Arrogant." She smirks.

"Ladies and gentleman," the singer from the band announces into the microphone. "Please welcome onto the dance floor, for the first time, Mr. and Mrs. Finn Jagger."

I offer Ashley my hand and she takes it in hers as I lead her onto the dance floor that has been laid over the grass.

The guests disperse from the area to stand around watching as I take Ashley into my arms and begin to move her across the floor. Glasses clink all around us.

Ashley smiles at me as I lean in to give the people what they want. Our lips touch and for just a second, I'm back upstairs in the bedroom with Ashley, but this time, I keep my wits about me, keeping it firmly in my mind that we're not alone and this time I can't drag Ashley away.

I pull back from kissing Ashley. She's still flushed and her eyes are shining like never before. I realize it's going to be hard keeping the promise I've just made myself that I'm not going to whisk her back upstairs, especially if she keeps pressing herself against me like this.

I smile and wave my arm, beckoning other people onto the dance floor. Ashley giggles in my arms as I twirl her faster as our guests begin to join us on the dance floor.

This day was always going to go one of two ways. Either Ashley would not show up and it would be the worst day of my life. Or Ashley shows up and it becomes the best day of my life. I don't know how I got so lucky, but I'm so pleased it turned out to be the best day of my entire life.

24

ASHLEY

I t's getting latish now, almost half past ten, and the party is still in full swing. The drinks have been flowing all day and all evening. Our guests are having a great time, dancing, laughing and chatting.

Finn and I have had to deny several assumptions that our quick wedding is because I'm pregnant which I'm not. The first few times, I tried to explain how it isn't the seventies anymore and if I were pregnant, it wouldn't necessarily be a reason for us to get married. The more I tried to explain, the more convinced people became that I was indeed pregnant. I've given up now, just letting Finn smile mysteriously and shake his head. There are a few people here tonight who are going to be disappointed in a few months' time when no baby comes.

I wonder how many of them would have been disappointed if no wedding had come at all. Something tells me only my guests, Finn's close friends and family would have cared. The rest of the guests would have loved it. It would have given them something to talk about for years to come.

That's not why I changed my mind and came though. I was telling Finn the truth earlier. At first, I wasn't planning on coming here today, but then I got to thinking, like *really* thinking. I knew if I didn't give us a chance, it would be the single biggest regret of my life, and no matter what came after it, I would always wonder what would have happened if I had just given Finn a chance.

Yes, he made a mistake, but when I let myself think about it rationally, I knew he'd done it with good intentions. He wasn't trying to control me, he hadn't even thought of it that way, he just didn't want to lose me. I knew I couldn't let us lose each other just because I was mad.

Finn has been in the bathroom and now I spot him walking back towards me. We're still outside. Lights and heaters have been set up around the edge of the event and it's beautiful out here, it really is, but Finn is grinning at me in a way that indicates we might not be out here for much longer, and I'm definitely on board with that.

As he gets closer to me, his smile slips a little.

I frown. "What's wrong?"

He sits down next to me and takes my hand in his. "Earlier Ashley, I promised you that I would never keep anything from you again. There is one more thing I've been hiding from you."

I feel my stomach turn over and a cold shiver runs through me.

Finn digs in his pocket and pulls out an envelope which he hands to me. "I hope you can forgive me."

I open the envelope, almost afraid of what I'm going to see. When I pull out the documents from inside, my jaw drops. "But this is—"

"Yeah," Finn interrupts.

"And we'd have to—"

"Yeah," he interrupts again.

"Finn, I really appreciate this, and the idea of flying off to Rome with you is just perfect. But you know I can't just go. The charity needs—"

"The charity is sorted. I've already spoken to Andrea. She's cleared your calendar and the day to day stuff, she'll be doing."

"I don't even have any clothes with me. Or my passport."

"Your mom organized both. Please just say you'll come on this honeymoon with me," Finn pleads.

"Fine." I sigh, then I laugh with delight. "Yes. Yes, I'll come. Thank you." I throw my arms around Finn. "Winding me up like that and letting me think it was some big secret that I might be mad about was a cruel joke," I laugh when I release him.

"It wasn't a joke. I really didn't know if you'd be mad I'd kept it from you after what we said earlier," he replies.

"Ok then, we need some ground rules. Anytime you wanna

fly me off to one of the most romantic cities in the world, I won't be mad if you keep it as a surprise." I grin.

"Got it." Finn nods.

"When do we leave?" I ask.

"Now."

I nod and stand up, noticing the area is suddenly empty. "Wow, people have cleared out quickly, haven't they?"

Finn grins at me.

I realize the grounds have cleared suspiciously quickly. "Another secret?" I giggle.

"Not so much," Finn says. "This is just a standard wedding thing."

"I'll give you that one." I take his hand.

We cut across the lobby of the hotel and step out of the front doors. We walk down the steps and through the tunnel of guests who throw confetti at us.

I don't feel like I'm just walking to a waiting car and going to the airport. I feel like I'm walking towards a whole new life.

EPILOGUE

F ive Years Later
   Finn

I smile proudly to myself as Ashley steps up to the front of the small crowd who is gathered in the dining room area of the new Jagger Center.

"Look, it's mommy!" Carla squeals excitedly from my side, pointing to Ashley.

"It sure is." I grin. "Listen to what she's about to say, okay?"

Carla nods and turns her focus to Ashley. Carla is three, a carbon copy of Ashley to look at. She even acts like her, she's quick to anger, but so loving, she definitely makes her decisions with her emotions. Reece, our nine month old son, sits in my arms gurgling away happily. He's more chilled out than Carla ever was as a baby. Maybe he's going to turn out to be more like me. Ashley insists he has my eyes, although I don't see it.

"Ladies and gentlemen," Ashley announces, a wide smile on her face. "Thank you all so much for being here today. As some of our top donors, I thought it only fitting to invite you to the opening day of the new Jagger Center, a place for homeless teens to get advice and help, but also to get so much more than that. It's also a place where they will get a hot meal, food to take away with them, and perhaps most important of all, a bed for the night in our dormitories. This place is going to make a huge difference to our community and it's going to show our youth that someone does care about them. That's a powerful message, especially when everything feels hopeless. So... thank you, each and every one of you, for making all of this possible. I now declare the Jagger Center officially open. Please do feel free to take a look around and ask any questions you might have." Ashley moves through the crowd to join me and the kids as a rapturous applause from the donors sounds through the room.

They are already beginning to move around and take a closer look at some of the facilities. Ashley only mentioned a few of the facilities, but there's also computers for the kids to use to apply for jobs or housing. And there's a book library too, so every kid can come here to lose themselves in a book and forget their troubles for a few hours.

Members of staff are already moving through the crowd, talking to the donors and answering any questions.

"God, was that speech as awful as I feel like it was?" Ashley asks as she takes Reece from me and holds him up in the air until he giggles.

I lean in and kiss her cheek. "Awful? No, it was perfect. Just like you."

"I don't feel very perfect." Ashley laughs, bringing Reece down to her hip where he contentedly blows spit bubbles. "I just keep waiting for something to go wrong."

"Nothing will go wrong," I assure her.

Carla tugs on Ashley's skirt and holds out a small dinosaur toy. "Nothing bad can happen. I have my lucky dinosaur," she announces.

"Oh see, I didn't know that." Ashley smiles. "But yeah, obviously, you're right."

"Hey, Finn. Ashley said you'd be here today. It's so good to see you," a young woman says as she comes up to us. She's wearing the red polo shirt and black pants that say she works at the center, but I don't think I've seen her before. Clearly, I must have though because she knows who I am. I study her for a moment. She looks vaguely familiar, but I still can't place her. Talk about embarrassing.

"You don't know who I am do you?" the woman asks.

I shake my head. "No. I'm sorry, I don't," I admit.

She laughs. "Oh, I'm taking that to be a good thing. I obviously don't look as rough as I did the last time we met," she says with a smirk.

Suddenly, it clicks into place who she is. "Gemma?"

"You got me." She laughs. "I've just finished my social work degree and Ashley offered me a job here."

"That's amazing, congratulations on the degree," I say. "And the new job."

She looks serious suddenly. "It's thanks in part to Ashley for getting me a place with a family who made me see I did have something to offer the world. But it's also in part thanks to you..."

I wave away her words and shake my head. "No way. It's because of you. You went out and did the work."

"I did. And I guess some of it comes down to me, but that day you saw me outside of Ashley's old office, you really *saw* me. And you showed me the world isn't always a bad place. So thank you. Not just for the room, but for seeing the human being instead of the problem."

"May I?" I ask, extending my arms.

"Of course." Gemma smiles, accepting my hug with a fierce hug of her own. She pulls back from me and smirks again, nodding to Ashley and the kids. "And I see it worked. It impressed her." She winks.

"Yeah, maybe I should be the one thanking you!" I chuckle.

Gemma spots a teenager in ragged clothes hanging around in the doorway to the center. "I have to go," she says. "But it was wonderful to see you again, Finn."

"You too," I respond, meaning it. It is so good to see how her life has turned around.

She flashes me one last smile and then she goes over to the kid in the doorway, ushering her in and chatting to her all of the time as she does it.

"You didn't tell me Gemma would be here," I glance at Ashley.

"She wanted to surprise you. I think she wanted you to see you made a good investment in her, that she really did take her second chance."

"She's really turned her life around." I nod. "But all I did was get her a hotel room. Really, the credit has to go to you for finding her a nice family and her for sticking in school and going the distance."

"How about we call it a team effort?" Ashley concedes.

"Yeah, I like the sound of that," I agree. I bend down, scoop Carla up into my arms then I sit her on my hip and wrap my arm around Ashley's shoulders.

We stand quietly for a moment as a family and I can't help but wonder, even now, how I got so lucky as to have this wonderful, selfless woman fall in love with me.

The End

COME SAY HELLO!

Thank you so much for reading!
Please click on the link below to receive info about my latest
releases and giveaways.
NEVER MISS A THING

Or
come and say hello here:

OTHER BOOKS

www.ingramcontent.com/pod-product-compliance
Lightning Source LLC
Chambersburg PA
CBHW022152170626
46807CB00005B/2172